Horsethief
Moon

Dan—
I think you understand horse
and baseball
will and

Best to you
and yours—
Jim

One Co Publishing

Horsethief
Moon

by

Jim McBride

One Co Publishing

Library of Congress Card Catalog Number:
TXu777-734

First Printing: September, 1997

Cover photo credits:
"Bareback Rider"- David R. Stoecklein
Inserts - Joan Kelly Lucason

Printed and distributed in the United States of America by One Co Publishing, P.O. Box 517, Oneco, Connecticut 06373, (860) 564-4839

Chapter I.

He was like a range cow and I was surprised when he returned. For a long time I had believed, like many others here in Window Rock, that the earth was flat and I thought it to be true because of all those who had ever left; he was the only one to ever come back.

We had been partners since our days in high school and we team roped in many rodeos and worked our way across the prairies through Arizona, Texas and New Mexico. And after many years he said to me. "I'm going east this Fall to see the Manhattan skyline and ride saddlebroncs in the Square Garden."

I would have liked to go with him, but my father, Henry Poorcrow was not well and I was afraid that I would panic when I got to the edge of the world.

Her name was Karen and she lived on the Long Island and raised two girls, Sarah and

1

Teresa and two milk cows, Irene and Isabelle. Each morning at 5 o'clock, before she went to her job in the city, she milked inside the barn. She hummed and sang away at milking time and again each Sunday at church where she played the organ with the long pipes and sang the old hymns.

Unfortunately, in matters concerning the heart she was not happy and because her relationship with her husband was eroding away, she had been sleeping with another man from her church. His name was Larry and his father owned a textile mill and spun yarn and wove cloth.

The members of the congregation called him the "Threadman" and it was apparent to everyone that he was not really a true Christian, but he was generous each Sunday during the collection and they needed the money. He had begun courting his neighbor's wife by traveling into the city where she worked as a waitress and leaving her embarrassingly large tips. Once he left her a twenty dollar bill for a piece of pie and coffee. He thought he could buy her and at that time she was just using him because sometimes anything that resembles love is better than nothing.

It was a Sunday afternoon and her girls were next door at the neighbor's house kicking a soccer ball onto the roof and running around the yard. From her front room she could see them through the north windows which were shaded by the round-bellied apple tree that grew alongside the front porch.

In the Spring the air would fill with the delicate blossoms and exotic fragrance. And in the Fall it's crown shimmered with color as the beautiful tree gave up its sweet apples, loved by the two girls who polished them like Christmas tree ornaments.

She had told the Threadman, the week before, that she no longer wanted to continue seeing him. Probably one of the reasons was that he had such a horrible voice. Each Sunday, as she played the hymns, she could hear his guttural wallowing above the others. She was embarrassed that those awful sounds, that burst loose from his throat, were made by a human being. Each time he pushed his bellowing above a hog's grunt she thought maybe God hadn't really meant for people to worship together.

He had never been able to satisfy her and she had become tired of being his hand. Deep inside she knew she was worth more than being someone else's masturbator, and lying there unfulfilled afterward, talking about how much he loved her was like listening to bad German music.

The Threadman had tried to talk her out of her decision. He was a rich man and thought he could pay for and get anything in life he wanted.

But to her credit, one of Karen's greatest assets had always been her resolve and ability to remain unperplexed after having had some interior dialogue with herself.

"I thought we had a future," he said, his voice knotted up like the rusted wick riser on an old lantern.

"That's, maybe, what you wanted to believe," she replied.

"I don't understand," he pleaded. "I know you don't love your husband."

She just looked at him.

"I'm not going to let you do this," he said.

"I don't think you have much choice, Larry," she said smiling slightly.

"Are you laughing at me?"

"I'm not laughing at you, Larry. It's just that I'm already raising two children and I'm not equipped to be your therapist."

"Is that what you think?"

"No, right now I'm thinking how blessed the blind and deaf are."

Sometimes she would not be able to hold in her inner voice and the words, bone-hard, would swell in her and burst forth. She was a feisty woman even then.

"You see, Larry," she said. "I know there are guilty stains upon my conscience, but I believe I've paid my penance. For the past year I not only slept with you on occasion, but week after week I listened to you torture music until even Pastor Coates' lengthiest sermons seemed more palatable."

Her words were not like the fine rain that comes in the spring, but like the downpour that comes out of nowhere and feeds the dried-up stream.

"I must admit, though, that the congregation never sang louder. So I guess I should thank you for that. And I think what you did for old Fred Matthews was wonderful. Last week your shouting of the words to "How Firm a Foundation" encouraged the other singers to raise their voices to drown you out. And when Fred, who hadn't sung a note in years. picked up a hymn book from the bench-back rack and started singing, I knew something unusual and special was happening."

"But it was okay when I took you and your kids to the tennis matches at Forest Hills or took you out to the most expensive restaurants in the city?"

"No one twisted your arm."

"You used me," he said becoming increasingly upset.

"No more than you used me."

"You can tell me whatever you want, Karen, but I know you loved me."

"No." she said calmly, "You're wrong."

There was a long silence. Then Karen repeated herself. "You're wrong. I never told you I loved you. There's no way. Anything you think was between us is ancient history."

"You're kidding me."

"Hello," she said almost curtly. "Do you have a tough time knowing whether something is true or imagined?"

It made him mad that he was helpless and already she had established a distance between them.

"I can't believe you would rather be with Gregory the rest of your life."

She was waiting for someone who could turn her life around, someone who could pull the rug out from under her feet and then set her in the right direction.

"Better than living in a bad dream," she replied.

"You'll be back" he said

She looked at him, saying nothing, but her thoughts were clearly implied through her look.

"When you're lonely again, you'll come back," he said, a smile starting to curl on his lip.

"I'll never be that lonely," she answered.

A lot had happened since that conversation six days ago, she thought as she watched her girls go running through the yards. It was hard to believe that they were growing so quickly. In a life that could very easily have been so empty, they filled her completely. She delighted in the simple pleasures the girls got from chasing a soccer ball between houses or walking out to the back field to play cowgirls with Irene and Isabelle.

Several minutes later three cars pulled into the driveway and parked near the barn. Her husband, Gregory, followed by Pastor Coates and the Threadman, walked past the apple tree and came up onto the front porch. She knew this would be a somewhat difficult afternoon and she would have to do some quick dancing. It amused her and seemed wonderfully witty to consider the fact that two of these men had been born with ridiculously small genitals.

7

Chapter II

They say he could have been a ball player, but his heart wasn't in it. He could throw the ball like an arrow and Coach Brock at A. S. U. wanted him to play, but he loved horses and the open range more.

He was my friend and he never thought of me as an Indian, or Chinaman, or even a Swede. He never thought of anyone as anything other than what they were.

For such a big man, Cody was very gentle. He had a soft spot and kindness in his heart for anyone who had seen rough times. He especially loved children, for he, himself, had been able to keep his own innocence.

He always took the time to say a few words to strangers, even those standing beside him waiting for a table at the restaurant where Karen worked. He was surprised that so many people in such a large city couldn't talk, but then again he was a stranger himself in a strange land.

Jim McBride

Looking out beneath his hat, he caught Karen's eye and then a smile as he stood there waiting for a table. His wranglers, hat, and boots didn't impress the other, more properly attired, customers who looked at him wondering where he had his Winchester or Colt hidden.

But he had been brought up sinew-tough, knowing that it's best to try to understand each other's quirks and ways, so he just grinned and shuffled on his heels and tipped his hat as people pushed on by.

Recognizing that he was like a fish out of water, Karen approached him smiling and asked humorously, "Table for one, Billy?"

"Billy?" he replied.

"You are Billy the Kid, aren't you?" she teased.

"No ma'am, Cody Stewart."

"Well, okay then, Mr. Stewart..."

"Cody, please, ma'am."

"Okay then, Cody, table for one?"

"Yes ma'am. It's just me and my shadow," he said looking back over his shoulder. "And he's a grub liner."

"Grub liner?"

"A cowhand who arrives just before supper and leaves before work."

Karen laughed.

"You know some grub liners?" he asked.

"Sounds a lot like my children."

"You have kids?"

"Two girls."

"How old?"

"Eleven and twelve."

"That's great!"

Later she brought him a cup of coffee and asked him where he was from.

"The west."

"How long have you been away from home?"

"A couple of weeks." Then after a moment he added how he had taken his time getting to New York. "I didn't want to push the pickup and I wanted to see some places I'd only read about as a kid."

"Like?"

"Louisville, Kentucky and Gettysburg."

There are many good qualities that a person can have, but living an uncomplicated life is probably one of the best. He had tried to do that. There had been a terrible thing that had happened in the past, but he tried not to think too much about it anymore. He had long ago ceased looking for something (that he had

11

no idea what it looked like) and he had replaced it with a plan.

He had been lucky with the rodeos and had been able to put some money away. When I talked to him about what he would do with the money he got a far-away look in his eyes, like the mustangs get when they have been run to the cut banks.

He had been able to replace everything that reminded him of Sara with something else. He had given away almost everything he owned and he believed the only thing remaining, her memory in his heart, would be enough to get him through. For Cody, pain was just the other side of feeling good.

They had been out dancing that night at the Dog House and she was very tired so she left in her own car to go home. He knew he should have driven her, or at least followed her to the edge of her father's ranch, but we were still having a good time and he didn't want us to see how great a handful of mane she had him by.

"More coffee?" Karen asked.

"Please ma'am."

It seemed to him that he amused her with the way he talked - calling her "ma'am" and being so polite. And he could tell by looking into her beautiful tawny-colored eyes that she was enjoying the conversation they'd begun. He knew that she was a woman who must have spent time out of doors because she still had some summer freckles around her nose and cheeks. And when she poured his coffee he saw that her hands had the look of a woman who knew what working for a living was all about. They were very clean, showing signs of endless scrubbing, by their roughness.

"I'll bet you've raised animals," he said to her with an appreciative smile.

"What makes you think that?" she replied.

"You've got good hands; those hands have probably given a pat of praise to a horse or some other creature."

"Cows," she said, then after a pause added, "I've got a couple of Guernseys."

"There you go."

She liked the simple and unconcealed delight he took in talking about things that excited him.

"I'll bet your cows even come over to you when you're around the fence," he said grinning.

Her eyes widened as he spoke of things that she knew happened and she was interested in how he was able to perceive it.

13

"It's a dead giveaway that someone's taken time with an animal if that animal will come up to them when they're around," he said. "Most critters are pretty smart and know what loyalty is about." Then he added, "That gift is more precious than many others, don't you think?"

She was enjoying her conversation with the cowboy. He seemed to be a man with no fine print, no hidden agenda.

It was nice to wait on someone who was not on some secret mission or being evasive as they flirted with you while their wives were at Macy's doing the Christmas shopping. She thought to herself that there was more substance behind this man from the west than he allowed her to see, but that was okay because he was refreshing.

He was unspoiled and untouched. He was one of those rare people you run into in life who develop strong friendships and work at keeping them. It was obvious that he had spent some time finding out about himself and he'd put what he'd found in clearly marked packages. What you saw is what you got.

She had given him a seat at the window where he could look out at the passersby. It was a crowded room and his chair had been pushed snugly into the wooden table. It was a far cry from the kitchen window back home that opened out on to the vast meadow which spread as far as the eye could see.

Around him he heard snatches of conversations of the customers who came into Morgan's to conduct their daily business.

"Would you like a bowl of soup?" Karen asked him. "It's good today."

"It wasn't good yesterday?" he teased.

"It's usually good everyday."

"What kind is it?"

"Cream of asparagus."

He winced.

"Ma'am," he said smiling broadly, "Without meaning to be disrespectful, I am sitting here in this fancy restaurant in New York City, wearing a cowboy hat and boots that have stepped in cowpies from as far as Phoenix to Cheyenne, and you're asking me if I'd like to try some asparagus soup?"

She laughed at him knowing that she was being deservedly kidded. But being the kind of woman who could give as well as she got, she replied, "About those boots, Billy. Maybe you should have checked them at the door along with your guns. They sound dangerous."

As she spoke, for an instant, she reminded him of someone he'd known before; but he put

15

the thought out of his mind and he turned and watched the crowds out on the street go by. For the first time in a long while he felt a loneliness come over him.

Karen brought him his meal. He had passed on the soup, denied the salad and refused any vegetable except the potatoes. He wanted two of those baked, no sour cream, just lots of butter and of course the largest steak they had - well done.

To his surprise it was a pretty large steak, not as big as the ones you could get at the Dog House, but still pretty big. He took the knife and cut into it as she refilled his coffee cup. There was still a hint of some red in the center of the steak and he said to her, "Ma'am if you call the vet quick, I think we can still save this one."

"It's not done well enough for you?"

"I'm just pulling your leg. It's fine," he laughed good naturedly.

Karen was not used to repressing her curiosity, especially with the people she waited on day after day; but she was kind of half embarrassed when she heard herself ask him what he was doing in the city.

"I'm riding bucking stock over at the Madison Square Garden," he responded politely.

"Bucking stock?"

"Saddle broncs," he answered.

"Isn't that dangerous?"

"Yes ma'am, but it's a great way to meet nurses."

"Or doctors." Then after a second she humorously added, "Then again, maybe you're one of those Neanderthals that doesn't think a woman could be a doctor."

"You know something, ma'am? I like you; you remind me of someone I knew once, and she would always say things to correct me about the modern world things like, "toll booth person" not, "toll booth man" or, "flight attendant" not, "stewardess" and of course, "cowperson" not, "cowboy". He laughed at his own silliness and reassured her that he meant no harm.

Karen made her sweep through the dining room several times, coming back more often than usual to see how the cowboy was doing. They'd exchange a few barbs and laughter and then she'd move on. She knew with all that was going on in her life, the idea crossing her mind was instant insanity. Yet, she had enjoyed the past hour as much as any she'd had in a long time. She secretly hoped he might

17

return again for lunch or dinner before he left for good.

"When does the rodeo end?" she asked him as she came back to his table.

"Sunday afternoon."

"And then what? You saddle up old paint and ride off into the sunset?"

"No ma'am. I don't have old paint with me this trip. It's just Cody and the pickup," he said taking a glimpse into her eyes and swallowing a shy grin.

"Some dessert?" she asked, her eyes brightening. "The pie's good today." Then she quickly added, "And it was good yesterday and the day before, Lemon meringue. You'll like it."

"I don't think so. Thank you anyway."

"Really?"

"No, no pie today."

She wasn't sure what was happening, but it was, and she found herself saying a moment later, in her best Calamity Jane imitation, "I don't believe you heard me, stranger. I said I'd like you to try the lemon meringue pie."

His eyes narrowed and he looked her straight in the eyes. "I ain't scared of you, Missy," he said in his best John Wayne.

"Go ahead, make my pie."

Then he laughed. And Karen laughed. And a family at the next table turned to see what was going on. He tipped his hat to them and said he was sorry to have disturbed them. Then he pushed back his chair and stretched out his legs beneath the table and they laughed some more.

It felt good to laugh again with someone else. The guys behind the chutes were okay; but this was better, hearing a woman's voice cracking up. He remembered how much fun he used to have, how much he used to laugh.

"I can tell that you like what you do," he said to her. "You seem pretty happy.

"Most of the time." Then almost as an apology she added, "But it's just a waitressing job."

"There's nothing wrong with that," he said sincerely. "You make a lot of people happy, and that's a good thing. Don't ever lose your kind feeling for people," he said.
"Thank you," she replied and she turned and smiled back at him as she walked across the room towards the kitchen.

For some reason when those words, "thank you" were spoken he caught in her eyes and face an expression that seemed to conceal

19

something. It was not anything he could put his finger on; it was just that those words seemed to have been said with a genuine appreciation, almost as if she weren't used to being paid real compliments.

Outside the crowds strolled home to their apartments or walked briskly by corner storefronts or loitered in front of the restaurant window waiting for a taxi.

There was a man waiting at the hostess station. He looked like a weasel peeking into the henhouse door and when he saw Karen entering from the kitchen with the pie, he approached her. In a comical, almost effeminate way, he leaned toward her as if trying to establish some type of physical dominance. His eyes were glistening and somewhat arrogant as if saying to her, "You have to listen to me because you're a little nobody and I feel contempt for you."

Cody could not hear what he was saying, but it was obvious that Karen was not happy with his being there. He looked like someone who had never raised a bead of sweat outside of a health club. There was something pathetic in his demeanor as he spoke and gestured turbulently. Karen, hoping to avoid an embarrassing scene, maneuvered him toward the rear of the room away from the customers.

From where he sat, Cody thought that the man reminded him of a lot of other men he'd run into in his life, that were all gurgle and no guts.

They talked for a few minutes and she appeared even more agitated as the man's words quickened something within her. He looked at her with a persistent stare and then with a contemptuous smirk he cruelly laughed at her.

She tried to move past him, back into the main dining area, but he blocked her way with his arm.

Suddenly she gestured slightly towards Cody, but her words to the man were concealed as the man stepped fully in front of her. Reflexively, Cody rose from his chair, but as he did the man stepped aside and let Karen reenter the dining room.

As she approached Cody with the pie, the man, camouflaged by the patrons around him, slipped back out into the street.

Karen placed the lemon meringue pie before the cowboy.

"Someone you overcharged?" he asked her lightly, trying to lessen what had been some difficult moments for her.

"No, just someone I know."

"I hope all the people you know don't

treat you like that," he said concerned.

"He's just a guy I played tennis with."

Cody had made it a point most of his life to mind his own business, especially with people he didn't know or strange places. And more and more this city known as "The Big Apple" was getting stranger and stranger. He did, however, at times, alter that decision when it came to friends old or new. Sometimes life could get complicated and those principles would not be rigidly adhered to. He had found that usually those changes came as a result of a sleepless night or a beer-aided evening; seldom, if ever, had his principles changed over a piece of lemon meringue pie.

"Ma'am, it's none of my business," he said. "And you can stop me right now and tell me that straight out, but you might want to try and find a better kind of a man to call 'friend'."

"I didn't say he was a friend," she responded. "I said I played tennis with him."

Cody grinned and said cautiously, "It looked to me like he was scoring most of the points."

She looked at him with one of those looks people get when they want to be mad about something, but know the person they want to be mad at doesn't really deserve it. Maybe it was because he was a cowboy and everybody loves a cowboy or because she would have liked to have the freedom to come and go as he did.

For Karen life had become "sameness". The sameness of black coffee, hot food, long drives into work and neon signs. Some people her age would look back on their lives and not want to change a thing. Karen wasn't one of them.

She loved her two girls and her life revolved around raising them properly and seeing to their needs. She had been able to provide everything from baby carriages to Cheerios and they in return gave back to her the only real love she'd received in many years.

In between the last bites of the pie Cody looked up from his plate at her. "Ma'am, I was as out of line as an affidavit at a liar's convention," he told her apologetically. Then he added, "Just because I have no money in my pockets doesn't mean I have the right to put my hands in yours, ma'am. So, I'm begging your pardon."

"Do I look like a school teacher to you?" she said smiling once again.

"Is this a trick question?" he asked, happy to see the smile. "If I get it wrong do I have to eat more pie?"

"You keep calling me 'Ma'am' and I keep thinking I'm some ninety year old school teacher in Texas," she said humorously.

"My name is Karen and I'm sure where you come from 'ma'am' is meant with the greatest respect, but around here it sort of means wrinkles and gray hairs." Then after a pause she added, "Maybe, then again, that's what you do mean."

"No ma'am, I mean Karen. There's no disrespect intended and I'll try not to let it happen again. Sometimes though, I find it hard to break old habits. I'm one of those fellows that if you threw me into the river I'd naturally float up stream."

She enjoyed talking with him. It was difficult not to like him because he laughed a lot; it was not the false kind of laughing she heard from the three piece suited crowd, but the, "I can laugh at me because I don't think I'm too smart or take myself too seriously," kind of laughing.

When a man lives by himself he gets into certain habits as far as eating, cleaning and sleeping are concerned. Cody was the type of man who would naturally clean up his plate after eating and take care of whatever gear was involved with the meal. Any leftovers would be relegated to his cowdog, Tom, who never quite got the hang of being well-mannered and respectful with humans. But for Cody, he was affectionate good company who played rough, without meanness, and was as loyal as Lassie.

Cody had thought of bringing Tom east with him, but not knowing what to expect in a city the size of New York, he ruled it out. And it was a good thing too, as Tom's dark side would not have gone over very well. The city was already too gloomy.

He had hoped that the trip east would also help him come to terms with Sara's death. Even though it had been over three years since it happened, there wasn't a day that went by that he didn't see her somewhere in the landscape. And now in the concrete canyons of New York he found that each night the same dream mechanically came back into his head. Sometimes in the early morning hours, hoping to hold off the dream, he would try and convince himself that he should not have loved her so much in the first place. He tried to make himself believe that that would be the easiest place to start to dull her memory, but he was wrong, because even now he was meeting someone who reminded him of her.

"Is there anything else I can get you?" Karen asked drawing him back from his reverie.

"I guess I'm all set," he replied.

"I'll be right back with your check."

"What's that?" he said as a grin broke out across his face and he began to laugh.

"What is it?" she asked.

"I'm sorry," he said. "I thought for a half moment that you said you'd be right back with my stick, and I imagined my dog talking to me about a stick I'd thrown."

"That is pretty funny. What kind of dog is he?" she asked, not wanting the afternoon's conversation to end.

"Cowdog."

"He's part cow?" she laughed. "Does he mind being milked?"

"No, but he hates it when I put mustard or chili on him."

They both laughed once more and the family at the next table looked over at them disdainfully.

"Actually, he's a great old black and white collie I use for finding strays. He's a great tracker; he can find anyone or anything. It's been a long two weeks not having him around. He was like my shadow.

"I'll bet he misses you a lot," Karen said. Then trolling for some more insight into the cowboy's life she asked, "You have someone taking care of him while you're away?"

"My partner, Poorcrow. He'll keep Tom in line."

"Is he an Indian?" she asked.

"Cowdog," he laughed trying to be funny.

"I meant your partner," she said amusedly.

"Navajo." Then he added, "And he doesn't like mustard or chili on his back either."

They both smiled at each other.

"Billy's the only man on earth that Tom's afraid of," Cody said. "One day he chased him down the road with a chainsaw and ever since then Tom has given him a wide circle."

Then pushing himself away from the table and rising from his chair he said, "I guess I'd better be going. Eight o'clock will be coming around soon enough and I'm sure there's some very rank horse waiting with my name on his dirt list."

He took a look at the check and then pulled enough money out of his pocket to cover it and the tip. He moved in front of the window cutting off the light that had been filtering into the room.

"Well, Karen," he said, "I appreciate the good conversation we've had. You've had a lot of patience."

She stood there, still, half smiling, with her hands by her side.

"This has been one of the best meals I've had. I'm only sorry I didn't find out about Morgan's sooner. Then he added kiddingly, "If I'm still in one piece, I'll most likely stop by tomorrow for lunch again. So, I'll see you then."

"You won't be able to do that," she replied softly. He looked at her quizzically.

"I take that back. You'll only be able to do part of that."

"How's that?"

"Tomorrow's my day off."

"Oh, that's too bad." Then correcting himself he said, "I mean, it's not too bad that you have a day off, it's...well, I mean, I enjoyed talking with you...So if you have the day off...I must sound a little goofy, huh?"

"No, no, believe me, I have heard goofy before and you're not even close."

He looked at her and saw in her so much of Sara. He would have liked to tell her that, but he had no idea how to go about it. "What do you say to someone who reminds you of a woman you used to love, a woman who was now dead," he thought to himself.

The way she walked, carried herself, easily and beautifully, was so similar. There had been hints of Sara in other women he had met over the years, but now, here in New York City he realized they had all been only poor imitations.

Cody had built within himself a stillness and sanctuary that he retreated to whenever Sara's memory overwhelmed him. When he thought of her too much his soul ached; it became heavy and tired and he wanted to sleep. Maybe it was because when he slept he was with her again.

"Thank you," he said warmly. Then continuing he said, "I usually mind my own business and don't say too much most of the time; so, I hope you'll forgive my rattling on this afternoon, and anything I might have said to offend you."

"You haven't offended me and to use one of your words, I 'appreciate' the concern you showed a while ago. It's nice to know there are still some men out there that are capable of being sensitive as well as determined."

Cody tipped his hat somewhat embarrassed by her unexpected kind words.

"I'd better be going," he said, "because this is sort of where the pack mule gets too close to the ledge."

"I'm not sure I know what you mean," she replied.

Of the few talents he had, being faithful to people and memories was one of his best, and rather than make a fool of himself he just made a joke about his pack mule comment.

"Sometimes I've been known to make a real jackass out of myself," he said lightly, "so I'd better just move on. Thank you again for as fine an afternoon as I've had in a while."

He held out his hand and taking hers he gave it a strong squeeze. Karen's hand was firm, long and slender, and it felt good holding it for that second or two before he walked out the door into the crowded city.

Chapter III

The buzzer sounded and the first eight seconds, which were the easiest of that go 'round, were over. But the next four were the toughest. As he released the braided rein and reached to grab hold of the pick up man's waist "Weather Beater" lunged and jerked to the left. Then he dived and his front landing legs buckled beneath him, taking Cody to the ground with him. The panicking horse rolled over kicking wildly to get up, catching Cody several times on the thigh.

Half scrambling, half crawling Cody headed towards the chutes as one of the pick up men chased the bronc through the gate. He heard the announcer give out his score as he limp-walked along the chutes, past the tight-lipped cowboys waiting for their next event. He felt the numbness around his thigh increasing and he knew his leg was skinned up pretty good.

He braced himself against the top rail of

the fencing as he made his way toward the rear of the arena. He used to cuss a lot when wrecks like that happened to him, but found that it became too easy, and pretty soon just about every other word out of his mouth was a cuss word. So one day, I think it was at a little rodeo in Peabody, Kansas, he decided to stop. He told me that he didn't want anything to have control over him: not horses, not women, not words; and that's why when he didn't score well in an event, he was a hard person to be with.

Sometimes we would drive two or three hundred miles after an unacceptable performance, and he would never say a word. I, myself, liked the other Cody better, the one who used to cuss the whole way. I think maybe once in a while he might've cussed to himself, but not in front of people, not in public anymore.

"Hey, Cowboy," he heard a familiar sounding voice call out to him. He turned and looked across the chutes. "It looked to me like the horse was scoring most of the points," the voice said, recalling to mind the words Cody had said earlier in the day at the restaurant.

"Hi," he half laughed back at Karen.

"Is there anyway I can get over there?" she asked.

"That's not a good idea," he said. "I'll

come around that far end in a few minutes. I'll meet up with you there."

So Cody collected his saddle and equipment, assured the medical people as he checked out, that he was okay, and went off to meet the young woman from Morgan's.

Karen was waiting for him She had on real clothes, not the contrived waitressing outfit the restaurant required. She looked at him and her eyes sparkled with genuine interest.

"Are you okay?" she asked seeing him trying to walk naturally, but in obvious discomfort.

"Sure," he said. Then he added, "My leg's just not used to being a horseshoe pitching pin."

Trying to continue with the humor he started Karen said, "I thought the idea was that you were to sit on the horse, not vice versa?"

"Well, sometimes if you really want a big score, you give the bronc his chance. You noticed though he didn't stay on for the full eight."

He was having trouble negotiating his equipment bag and walking, so she put her shoulder under his arm, giving him some support. Beneath his pant leg his skin felt like it was covered with glue. And he thought that the stiffness was what was probably keeping it

33

from collapsing.

"What brought you here tonight?" he asked, happy because for him it was a heartfelt need. "There must be a lot of other things you could have been doing?"

"I didn't think it was fair that you got to watch me work all afternoon, so I decided to see exactly what this rodeo business is all about," she told him.

"And?"

"I feel sorry for the animals."

"Listen, Karen," he said. "These animals are treated better than a lot of people. That horse, 'Weather Beater', that dumped me tonight, well, he works twice a week at eight seconds a shot. So, for sixteen seconds a week he gets the best feed and treatment that most animals would love to have. And do you know what's going to happen to him when he gets too old?"

"The glue factory?" she interjected.

"Dog food heaven?"

"That's cute," he replied. "If I wanted to be mean I'd tell you he'll wind up on Morgan's menu, but that wouldn't be the truth. The truth is that he'll be put out to pasture with a bunch of mares and die happy."

Out in front of the Garden a cab driver

put Cody's stuff into the trunk.

"Where to?" he asked the cowboy.

"The Hotel Earle, Washington Square."

Cody grimaced slightly as he slid into the back seat of the cab. Karen edged in next to him. He looked at her and saw a kindheartedness that he had missed in women.

"I'm just returning a rescue," she said with a peaceful smile seeing that he wasn't sure what was going on.

"What rescue?" he asked. Then he thought to himself, "Don't think about it, just be glad she's here."

After a moment he said to her, "Do you think we could make a stop?"

"Where?"

"Any place I can pick up a wooden leg and a parrot," he laughed.

"Thinking of changing occupations?"

"Well, I'd really like to get into something a little more dangerous. Maybe pirating would be nice; shiver some timbers or batten down a couple of hatches here or there," he chuckled. "Any idea how you shiver timbers?"

"Use lots of ice?" she responded.

They continued to joke as the cab made its way towards the end of the island. The laughter actually made him feel pretty good and it took his mind off of his leg. Around them the night was lit up by every type of neon sign imaginable.

The Hotel Earle was located at the corner of Fourth Street near the edge of Washington Square. As they got out of the cab they could hear music coming from inside the park and see chess players gathered around tables playing out matches. For a mid October evening it was still warm. The Indian summer had not yet stepped aside to let the coming coolness in or drive the street musicians out.

Cody paid the fare and with three good legs between them they got his equipment into the hotel.

"You're probably wondering why I chose this particular place to stay at," he said to her. And before she could answer he continued. "I remember reading about Gerde's Folk City, where Dylan first started out. I knew it was down here somewhere, so I decided I had to check it out."

The lobby was lifeless.

"You like him?" she asked as they stepped into the elevator.

"I always liked a couple of songs on his 'Nashville Skyline' album," he replied. And as I mentioned before, one of the things I wanted to do with this trip east was to see places that intrigued me. And Gerde's was one of them."

They got to his room and they put the equipment bag and saddle down in the hallway.

"I'd like to offer you a merit badge ma'am..."

"Karen." she interrupted.

"I'd like to offer you a merit badge, Karen, for helping me with everything tonight, but I think I'm plum out of them."

When he had finished he saw that she was looking at him with serenity.

"You'd better let me take a look at that leg," she said. "Don't worry, cowboy, I don't have any devious plans, I'm just paying you back for the rescue."

"You mentioned that before," he said opening the door. "But I'm not really sure that I know what you mean."

It was not the nicest room or the worst room he had ever stayed in. God knows that he'd been in some pits before. There were cigarette burns on the desk top and the little sofa below the window had been rained on and could have used a new cover. Basically though, it was clean and inoffensive.

He had tried when Sara died not to let her death terminate who he was, but as the weeks and then months had passed, his life became as different as he could have ever imagined.

They say that that is not an unusual reaction for someone who has lost so much, and Cody's depression was looked upon as just a period of adjustment by many of his friends. But, because he was my partner, I knew that he missed the comfort she had been able to give him all those years.

He still carried with him the first love letter she had ever written to him. She wrote it for him for his birthday. Each night before he went to sleep, no matter where we were on the road, he would take it out and reread it.

He came out of the bathroom wearing a P. R. C. A. tee shirt and a pair of gym shorts. His left thigh had been bruised pretty good and the muscle had tightened up, but the pain had subdued considerably. Blood had risen to the surface and needed to be cleaned up.

He limped over and sat on the sofa stretching out his leg across a small coffee table. Karen dampened a wash cloth and started to remove the thin film of dried blood along the wound.

"You should keep it elevated," she said

putting a pillow beneath his leg.

"I'll have to get you some ice too."

"How come you know so much about this stuff?" Cody asked her.

"Two soccer players at home," she answered. "Happens all the time, mostly ankles. Nothing that a couple of cupcakes, ice cubes and hugs won't cure."

He had to smile. She was remarkably alivé and there was a magical warmth in the way she spoke about her kids.

"They sound like fine children," he said.

Within his heart he knew that this was something he had missed out on. He had often thought about what kind of father he might have been. Sometimes women friends had visited him out on his small ranch and he was fond of them, but in the end he was still in love with Sara and the women who came, although welcomed, knew that this was so.

Karen sat down next to him on the sofa. "Sometimes a person will do something to make a situation a little bit more tolerable," she said.

Cody looked at her. He could see that whatever she wanted to say was important to her.

"This afternoon, when I was talking with the tennis player, I told him something so that he would leave me alone. I've never been too good at getting myself out of corners I've painted myself into," she said. "So...well...I feel very stupid now talking about this, but," she paused trying to get over the words, "I told him I was having an affair with you."

She admitted it to Cody without blinking her eyes. She looked right at him with all her vulnerability right out on the surface. He could sense the anxiety and uneasiness in her eyes.

"After I said it, I knew it was wrong. I knew I could have taken it back, and told him to leave me alone, but I knew he'd never accept it. He's one of those men that thinks he has to win, has to be right and won't be pushed away."

Karen was relieved.

"You're lucky you don't have warts," Cody said.

"Warts?"

"What's-his-name is a reptile isn't he? Do you think he'll leave you alone now?"

"Oh, he'll be jealous, but I don't think he'll press it anymore."

"How about your husband? Why not tell him the guy's been chasing after you?"

She looked at Cody and he knew the answer that was coming.

"Because it's been more than chasing," she said ashamedly.

"So telling your husband's not the best alternative."

"I guess you turned out to be the only one I had at the time. I never expected that he would come to the restaurant," she said softly. Then turning her head she looked out the window at the people in the square below.

"Well, the most important thing, as far as I can see it, is that you have a right to make whatever choices you want concerning your life. And they should be your choices; nobody should be allowed to throw a loop around your neck if you don't want it."

When she turned back to him, away from the window, there was moisture in her eyes although nothing suggested she was crying.

At that time she said, "It's not that I'm confused or anything, or even upset, It's just that I recognized what I was doing and the whole business kind of became repulsive. I didn't even like the guy. A few months ago, July I think, I started playing tennis with him and pretty soon I wasn't just playing tennis. I slept with him. Now I realize I don't care, actually never cared about him and I don't want my girls to be hurt by some crazy nonsense that might blow up in our faces."

Cody thought to himself that there were many fine qualities that this woman possessed. He knew she was a complicated, charming person and he cared that she had troubles. Maybe he was being foolish, but maybe it was right and necessary to offer her some kind of help.

"Karen," he said. "You ever been to the airport?" he asked smiling.

She looked at him like a child might look when being introduced to a new game.

"Of course," she replied.

"You know they have those sky caps that have the flatbed carts for your luggage?"

"Uh huh."

"And if you give them two or three bucks they'll put your bags on the cart and push it to the airline for you. Well, I think you have to pack up your Touristers, your Ralph Lauren's and even your carry on bags and put them on the plane while you run off in the other direction.

"I get the picture," she said.

"I don't mean it in any bad way," he continued. "I just have this thing about figuring out how to get the best out of your life. No matter what kind of situation anyone winds up in, good can come from it."

"Always?" she asked.

"Sure. Take a man who has lost everything. He has no family, no home, no pets, no friends, even no food. Perhaps he can live off of others, relatives, parents, deposit bottles and cans found along the highway, even some kind of work. But what if nothing turns up for him, what can he do?

Well, say he tries fasting. He has no food, so it becomes easy for him, and low and behold after a few days, through his fasting a light goes off in his head. Somehow, through his patience and determination, he finds a way to understand what's important to him. Soon after that he finds a pencil or pen or crayon and he makes a list."

"What kind of list?"

"I don't know. A list. It doesn't really matter what's on the list because what it all comes down to is that it's a start. And as long as anyone is willing to make a start he's never at the end."

Karen was pleased that she had become acquainted with the cowboy. She felt that he sincerely wanted her to take a step back, turn away, and stop looking at her life as an onlooker might look at a train derailment.

"You're not too mad then about what I said about you and I this afternoon?" she asked him.

43

"I used to ride fence and sometimes even in late spring, a quick snowstorm could blow in from the northwest," he said. "And because there were some well placed lineshacks out there, I'd be able to find shelter. Those lineshacks had food and wood in them because someone cared to provide for the next guy who'd need its use. I don't think offering a hand to someone in need is ever a bad thing."

She looked at Cody with warmth and kindness in her eyes.

"Besides, I don't even know the Toadman," he laughed.

"We call him the 'Threadman'. His family is involved with textiles," she explained with a slightly nervous edge to her voice. She knew that her relationship with the Threadman began because she was trying very hard to forget something she already knew, but wished she didn't: that her marriage to Gregory had deteriorated many years ago. The honest-to-God truth was that she had been living in a house filled with unreasonable arguments and a profusion of humiliation. Nothing she did seemed to please her husband and no matter how hard she had tried, she could not make him happy.

"Some people fall in love with someone because they think they know who they are. When I married my husband I was nineteen years old; I had completed two years of college and was pregnant. I thought Gregory was everything I could ever want in a man. I believed I was what he wanted in a woman. But as the years rolled by, day by day, he began removing my insides and stuffing somebody else into me, to make me into what he wanted."

Karen felt comfortable talking to Cody. She didn't know why except she suspected it had something to do with the fact that he was a listener. It wasn't about sex or yearning, but a try at understanding. It was nice and even pleasant because there was no awkwardness. She felt she could say what she was feeling and he actually paid attention without being judgmental.

"A few days ago I told Larry, The Threadman, that I didn't want to see him anymore. We had some verbal fisticuffs, but I thought I had made my point. That's why I was so surprised when he showed up at Morgan's today. He laughed when I told him I wanted to try and work things out with my husband. He didn't believe me. That's when I told him there was someone else, and you just happened to be the lucky guy sitting next to the window at table eight.

"This is the first time I've ever won any type of lottery," Cody said, a smile breaking out mischievously across his face. "I wish you had told me; we could have given him something to really think about."

Smiling with relief Karen said, "I can see that you've done some rescuing before."

"It wasn't really because I was at table eight, I hope," the cowboy said.

"When you first came into Morgan's there was an enormously fat man sitting a couple of tables to your left finishing his second hot fudge sundae. Do you remember him?"

"Kind of hard to miss."

"If he hadn't gotten up and left I'm afraid I would have chosen him. The man's a power eater. Every day he comes in here for lunch and has the same meal: steak and baked potato and two hot fudge sundaes for dessert. He can consume. I hope you're not offended," she said smiling.

"Offended? I was attracted to him myself."

They both laughed.

"I really don't know what would have happened if you weren't there this afternoon."

"I guess you would have gotten wet paint all over your shoes trying to get out of the corner."

He was grinning; there weren't too many men that she knew who still grinned. He wasn't offended by anything she had told him. He wasn't trying to be interesting; he was interesting. He wasn't trying to prove anything; he had nothing to prove. She found that, looking back at that moment in the afternoon, that for a split second, when she looked across the room at him, she could have pretended to herself that what she told the Threadman might have been true.

"I guess that's why they have paint remover," he said.

"I have to admit I've used my share. I usually get more of me than my shoes covered. There have been some corners I've rolled out of."

Karen considered what she had been saying. Then she said, "I don't know what I mean by that. If anything, I usually come out of tight spots pretty good."

Cody laughed warmly. "Is that boasting or the truth?"

"Indisputably, neither," she replied smiling.

"You laugh good, Karen. And that's good because nothing in this life comes free except laughter."

47

"Would you believe me if I told you that this afternoon and now, tonight, is the most I've laughed in quite a while."

"No, because I've seen hot fudge sauce on the face of the power eater at Morgan's, and he's got to make you at least chuckle once a day."

"Do you always try to have fun?" she asked.

"Fun? If that's what it's called, I've been doing it unintentionally."

"You certainly seem to be happy with yourself."

"That's only inside and outside. Around me is miserable," he laughed.

"Then I've made a big mistake," she said.

"What's that?"

"I should have been a cowboy."

"I don't think your husband would appreciate that."

"No more than he would appreciate what I was up to with the Threadman."

"Sorry, I didn't mean..."

"It doesn't matter. It's just too bad that nothing can ever happen to be better than the dreams you start out with." she said.

It was still for a moment as he looked at

her.

Then he said to her, "I learned somewhere along the line that starting out being pretty simple and stupid is when I've learned the most intelligent lessons." Smiling he added, "And there's never been an intelligent lesson I haven't turned stupid on either."

"When I first got married I thought the sky would be the limit. I didn't realize I'd have to do it on homemade wings," she said.

"At least you had the wings. The closest I ever got to flying was going over the head of a horse called 'Orville Wright' in Tulsa, Oklahoma.

Karen laughed.

"What was even funnier was that I had the same horse a few weeks later in Texas and I couldn't get off of him. He was a runner and after the first jump out of the chute he ran around the arena nonstop. I was on him so long they figured we were engaged and about to go shopping for furniture."

Karen liked the way he turned things into humor. He didn't mind making fun of himself and he didn't seem to take his pleasant blue eyes or infectious smile too seriously.

"I imagine you must like living in the city," Cody said to her.

"Where I live, believe it or not, is not like this. There are more close-growing trees than homes and a pretty good amount of space."

"That's right," he replied. "I almost forgot about your cows."

"A few years ago I found this rambling old house out on the island and luckily between our two incomes we were able to afford it."

She looked at him and he could see that her words stirred up some smoldering unpleasantness.

"At one time in his life Gregory had aspirations of becoming a writer, but with a baby born, early in our marriage, he took a high school teaching position. As time went by and my second daughter came along, his frustrations grew. Seeing himself locked into teaching grammar forever, he became hard and surly."

Karen walked across the room to where a coffee maker was set up.

"Do you mind if I help myself?" she asked.

"Sure, go ahead."

She added some coffee to the filter and then poured in some water.

Getting up, gingerly, Cody said, "I think I should see how this leg is doing." He took a couple of steps and it felt pretty good.

"You've done a good job with the rescue. I'll have to put the wooden leg on hold."

"Would you like any?" Karen asked offering to make him a cup.

"Please."

"Black?"

"Yes."

She made the coffees and returned to the small sofa.

"Won't your girls be looking for you tonight?"

"They're at their friends' for the usual Friday night sleepover. I called before I left work to make sure they got there okay."

"It must be hard making all those kinds of arrangements," he said.

"Thank God for school bus drivers and good neighbors." Then after a moment she added, "I'm glad your leg is all right and again, thanks for the listening and the understanding."

"You know Karen, there are many different kinds of horses out where I come from and it's possible to trade one type for another. No one has to ride the same one forever, especially if he turns bad."

Here he was giving her off-handed wisdom and he himself couldn't get through his own problems.

"It's not too hard to comprehend that some horses, like some men - Toadman Reptile - Threadman Textile, or whatever, won't carry you over the steepest terrain. Instead they'll fail you when the work's to be done. You'd be better off putting your faith in the animal that'll take you to the highest ridge, not the one who'd rather spend his life in the feed lot like some old fat banker."

She did not answer and then after a few moments' hesitation he said, "I guess maybe this is the second time today I've been out of line."

Karen smiled at his discomfiture. "You don't have to apologize," she said as neon light from the Earle sign outside the window pricked it's way into the room. The beige wall fetched the rays and held them in a relaxed grasp until Cody moved in front of the window eclipsing the light.

It was a dumb thing to have said. What right did he have to make comment on someone else's life. He walked over to her and took hold of her arm. He knew he could hurt her and he didn't want to do that.

"I'm truly sorry," he said.

He turned and stepped back to the window and looked out at the sky scrapers dulled against the night sky. He knew that back home the moon was starting its rise above the limestone hills. He stood there with his back toward her.

"Hey, it's okay, cowboy."

"No offense meant," he said turning to her.

"None taken," she replied.

Then he said almost solemnly and sentimentally, "You know one of the things I just realized that I miss from back home?"

"Your oil well?" she laughed.

"I don't have an oil well."

"I give up then. What?"

"The moon," he said. "There's no moon in New York City."

He wished he could see it because it had always made him cool and clear within himself. And it always brought with it pleasant memories, easily and naturally, like light coming out of a projectionist's booth.

"But you know there is one out there, even if you can't see it," Karen said quietly.

He had learned a long time ago about the consequences of a horsethief moon. He remembered how he would carry Sara on his back through the poison ivy to the edge of Bailey

Pond. But no matter how hard she tried to avoid it, she would always come down with "the itch".

She used to climb up on his back holding a six pack of Coors, some sandwiches and a blanket, and she'd ride him to the swimming hole.

When he thought of them: the times so long back, when they laid looking at the moon, he knew how everything else in the world was so unimportant. He remembered how much they loved each other and how impossible it had been to get along without her, and how terrible it had become missing her.

"Do you have someone back home?" she asked him innocently.

"No, I don't," he said. "There was a girl once, a woman, I mean, and I should have protected her more than anything else in the world, but I didn't." After a moment he added, "She died a few years ago in an automobile accident."

"I'm sorry," she said kindly.

He felt relieved that he was able to speak to someone like Karen about Sara. He was happy to be sitting in that dim room talking to this woman who reminded him of her.

As beams of neon moon filtered into the room, he said, "I'd be lying if I said I didn't miss her, We just had too little time."

"Sometimes a little is enough," she said hesitantly, smoothing away the hair from her forehead.

He continued in the same even tone.

"Maybe some people might think I was very lucky to have had someone to love, even for the smallest amount of time, but it wasn't enough. And when it's all over for me down here and I finally get to meet up with the Head Honcho, I'm going to look him straight in the eye and I'm going to ask him why. Maybe he'll just put me on the back of the fieriest, baddest bronc He's got and ride me down to Hell, but I am going to ask Him."

After Sara's funeral Cody had a very difficult time getting on. Somewhere inside of him a voice had said, "You might as well forget about sleep because you'll never have dreams that will make you happy." But when he did sleep he had wonderful dreams because he was with her again, doing over and over the things they did when she was alive.

Soon he was sleepy all the time and useless to himself and everyone else. He had become as useful as a one-legged man at a kicking contest.

In his dreams Cody rode to Sara's father's

ranch as often as a goose goes barefooted. In his dreams he sat with her in his pickup and talked about what their future together would be like. In his dreams he made love to her under the rustler's moon at Bailey's Pond.

"At the very least, maybe God will call you out on the streets of Laraedo at high noon," she said hoping to turn the conversation a little more cheerful. "What kind of advantage could He have after all: fast as greased lightening, on speaking terms with everybody He's already put in Boot Hill, or perhaps He packs a six shooter that sounds like thunder?"

Cody listened with amazement. Every time a blackness crept up on him and started to take hold, Karen relieved him of the burden with humor. He enjoyed knowing he amused her too.

"This is pretty grave business," he said jokingly. "But as far as gunfights or shootouts I'm allergic to lead.

"Maybe you'll just break out in a fit of c-o-f-f-i-n."

"You know what I like about your humor Karen? It's about as dry as the dust in a mummy's pocket."

Behind him he heard the window curtains flick against the wall, fluttering on a current of wind from outside. They would lift and nudge faintly forward on each wafting breath.

Karen was smiling, but the expression was more comfortable than just a smile. He saw it, caught there for a half-moment, before it became elusive and vanished.

"There are two things I like about you cowboy," she said in a tone that sounded almost wistful. "The first is that you are so naturally polite it's scary. The second is that you have the most truthful eyes I've seen in a long time."

"Thank you," he said, "But let me assure you you're not getting a really truthful version."

"Is there such a thing anymore as a truthful virgin?" she asked. "Or do you just have an aversion to truthful virgins?"

"You are quick, Karen, very quick. And I'm about three steps behind your 'two step'", he replied. He looked at her for a moment then said, "I used to be rude, sarcastic and irritable because I was kind of bitter about things. Then I realized that because I was suffering wasn't any reason to make others suffer."

Karen looked at him like she was trying to understand his mystery.

"I'm not a genius, but I know that having those friends who stuck by me, even when my blanket got bunched, helped me through my selfishness and miserableness. I put myself and them through a lot of punishment. There was a spell I did everything I could to bust open my head and burst open my heart. Believe me, if they didn't have such great concern they would have quit on me a long time ago."

He sat down on the sofa and braced his feet against the coffee table.

"It got so it wasn't any fun. Actually it was awful, friends thinking about you as sore or misunderstood. So I decided I'd get back to what I used to be, what was easy for me - and that's polite. It's probably the only thing in life I've never had to really work at."

"Well, let me tell you, Mr. Stewart, you do polite good," she smiled sheepishly.

"Thank you." Then he added, "See what I mean?"

He was an outdoors kind of man and he held his heart like a dipper over the waterbucket, afraid to get it wet, even though he was dying of thirst. He couldn't remember what it was like to spend the evening with a woman in a hotel room. It wasn't that he hadn't done it before, it was just that he was so snakebit he couldn't remember it.

Maybe it was cowardice, but as the hour approached midnight he knew he must let her go home. The warning signs were everywhere:

"Slow Down.", "This may be hazardous to your health.", "Dangerous Curve Ahead.", "Watch Your Step", "Speed Bump", "Fire Index Extremely High", "Ice Unsafe for Skating", "Do Not Engage While Engine Is Running." He knew he was capable of running through each one of them, but he feared the results would be bruised dreams and abrasions.

Before he could finish his thoughts she said, "I should be getting back to Morgan's and my car. It's getting late."

"I'm going to go down and check on the pick up," he replied. "I can get you back up town if you like."

"No, that's okay, cowboy. I have this thing for cab drivers too. It's gotten so I've learned a new language from every foreigner I've ridden with," she smiled amusingly. "I think you have to be from Pakistan or New Delhi to get a hack's license in New York these days."

Cody looked at her in silent amusement. Then he said, "Give me a chance to put on my jeans and I'll at least go downstairs with you."

"That's fine," she said. "Are you sure your leg's okay?"

"Feels good."

She sat down on the arm of the sofa as he

went into the bathroom and changed.

A few minutes later they walked out on to the square. Some mild excitement still came up from a few remaining chess players. Bits of isolated conversations slipped through, now and again, from over by the arch which reigned eminent amongst brownstones.

Across the square, near where his pick up was parked, an animal restlessly paced back and forth, its companionable shadow breaking up as it moved beneath a street light.

"Did you see that?" he said pointing out beyond the fountain and the partly concealing benches.

"What?" she asked as the creature disappeared at a slow trot down the sidewalk.

"For just a moment I thought I saw my dog, Tom, out there," he explained incredulously.

"I don't see anything," she said.

"Whatever it was, it's gone."

"You must have great eyesight...or imagination," she added.

"I can see far away real good," he admitted. "Up close, not so good."

"And imagination?"

"Not so good either."

They walked through the shadowy square toward the mouth of Fifth Avenue, where cut in alleys of reds, whites and yellows burgeoned forth, leaving a spray of glowing magic to illuminate her face. Her face was thin and delicate and the few thin lines around her green eyes were almost imperceptible. She was a beautiful woman.

Then something extraordinary happened. He found himself facing her, overwhelmed by what was unimaginable. He heard himself softly saying to her, "If you will be at work on Monday, maybe I'll stay till then."

He knew the "maybe" kept it all safe until he could read her reaction. He had not been intending to try to open any doors and certainly he was unsure of how she might respond to his whispered intention, but he knew he must see her again. Something was happening, but he wasn't quite sure what it was.

"Will that mess up your traveling plans?" she asked.

"The rodeo finishes up around four or five Sunday afternoon," he replied. "And I don't think I'd be much good at driving without another piece of lemon meringue pie," he laughed.

"I told you you'd like it."

"Then I'll be by for lunch Monday," he

said calmly.

"Great."

"So these were the feelings that had slipped away and almost disappeared over the past couple of years," he thought as they stepped off of the curb to cross the street. He enjoyed walking through the city, looking far ahead at the landscape that opened out around him, taking it all in with a quick passing glance. Many of the brownstones looked as though they had been built by the same builder. One was almost exactly the same as the other, strung side by side, encircling the square.

"It amazes me that people will live like this, on top of each other," he said edging closer to her.

Karen hesitated for a moment to look at the houses, as if she had never concerned herself with them before.

"Seems to me to be sort of like a stockyard for humans," he continued.

"They do save a lot of money on useless things," Karen said.

"Like?"

"Picks, shovels, garden tools," she replied.

"You're right," Cody said, "This is probably the only place in the world where you can measure your acreage in square inches."

"That's why it's called Washington Square," she said making a bad joke.

Fifth Avenue was busy with traffic and it was exciting walking in a city so alive at that hour. It did not take long before they spotted a taxi heading in their direction and Cody and Karen both stepped into the street and signaled the approaching driver.

The cab pulled up and Cody opened the back door for her. Karen slid inside and rolled the window down. She offered him her out-stretched hand.

"Thanks for being so nice," she said with more than kindness, knowing then how obvious she'd been.

"The pleasure's been mine, Karen," he said taking her hand.

For half a moment the warmth of her hand brought back a pleasant memory that had been off-limits to him until then. Like a wisp of music, full of nostalgia, he recalled a late afternoon with Sara at the edge of Bailey's Pond.

Karen's hand was delicate but strong and he couldn't help smiling as he released it, thinking how familiar it felt.

He gave the cab driver a ten dollar bill and told him to make sure she got to her car

okay. Then he turned and waved good-bye as
the cab pulled away from the curb.

"It's already Saturday morning," he
thought to himself as he started back towards
the hotel. "Another day and a half until I see
her again. That's not too bad."

Chapter IV

They came in off of the porch: Pastor Coates, followed by the Threadman and her husband, Gregory. Karen ushered them into the living room. Her first thought was to stick out her foot and trip the Threadman, hoping that he might go headfirst into the mantle over the fireplace, but on second thought she thought that would be too kind.

As each in his turn sat and faced her, she felt like the only piece of chum in a sea of sharks. She was headed around the corner on two wheels; she didn't want the blindfold or need a cigarette. She was on the high wire and the net below had a hole in it.

Larry, the Threadman, spoke first. "Karen, I asked Greg if I could come over this afternoon along with Pastor Coates because I'm afraid for my soul."

Karen knew what was coming. All he was really concerned with was hurting her

65

somehow, paying her back for rejecting him.

"I feel that the only way I can escape eternal damnation is by confessing here in front of Pastor Coates and Greg how much in love we've been."

Karen stared at his face in disbelief for several seconds and then she said, "You know, Larry, I keep looking at your nose expecting it to pop right out like Pinocchio's, but then I just remind myself, "Wooden nose: wooden heart. Both will burn very well in hell."

"Is what he's said true?" Gregory asked.

"No."

"Come on Karen," the Threadman interrupted.

"How much we've been in love Larry? Give me a break!"

"I'm worried about you and your soul too," the Threadman replied. "I know what I've done is wrong and I can only hope that God and Greg will forgive me."

"You'd better pray they will because I never will," Karen responded angrily.

"Karen, this is not like you," Pastor Coates interjected.

"Pastor Coates, I don't mean to offend you, but the only reason any of this is taking place today is because I told Larry here that I don't want anything to do with him anymore."

"So what he's said is true?" Greg broke in.

"No, it's not," she answered.

The wash had been hung out on the line and it still smelled. She wished she could reel it back in and wash it again, but to mix a metaphor, the horse was already out of the barn. And as everybody knows - you can lead a horse to water, but you can't make him saddle himself.

"What bothers me," the Threadman continued, "is that Karen told me the other day, she is having an affair with some cowboy she met somewhere or other. And I'm concerned about what that's going to do to you and your girls."

"This is great, just great," Greg interrupted. "I wasn't enough for you, not Larry neither? Now it's some cowboy!"

It was right out of "The Three Stooges". She had stepped over the line and was out of bounds. Her back was against the wall and her defenses were down. She was caught between the frying pan and the flame and the fat was in the fire.

"If I may interpose a couple of thoughts," Pastor Coates said almost reluctantly. "First we have to all get under control."

Jim McBride

The snowball was avalanching down the mountainside. The car's wheels were locked and it was skidding around a dangerous curve on black ice. And he advised control. Control? "You can't get that with hair spray," Karen thought, looking at the Pastor's slicked-back pompadour.

She had made her own bed, dug her own grave, and the rooster had come home to crow. She should have let the lying dog sleep and hoped that he might have drowned in the water passing under the bridge.

"I think it would be a good idea if Karen and I spoke privately," the Pastor explained. "Would you and Larry give us a few minutes alone please, Greg?"

"Do you really think it's necessary?" Gregory asked. "We all know what the story is here: my wife's been cheating on me."

"Please, Greg," Pastor Coates appealed.

"Okay, but it's against my better judgment."

The two men with the minuscule genitals left the room leaving Karen to speak alone with the pastor of her church.

"My job, Karen," he began, "is if possible, to help you and Greg get through this incident. Only you know what your present circumstances are and whether or not you want to try to save a marriage that has been dealt a severe blow."

"I'm not sure what I want at this point," she said. "I had been hoping for years that somehow, some way, Gregory would become his old self again, not the frenetic forty-year-old he has been. I've spent a good amount of my life feeding him, comforting him, even clothing him. He can't even pick out a matching shirt and tie, believe it or not.

Anyway, when he's not here, I get very accustomed to not having him around. When I realized a year or so ago I needed more from him and he didn't care, the possibility of turning elsewhere for support, understanding, love, etc. became appealing. My mistake is that this 'me' that was emerging put my faith in the Threadman."

"The Threadman?" Pastor Coates inquired.

"Larry, that's what we all call him in the congregation. Surely you know that?"

"Because of his singing?" the Pastor asked.

"It is kind of tightly wound, but that's not the reason; it's because of his business. His family spins yarn, makes textiles."

The Pastor was silent.

"What's really humorous about this...
and I don't know if any of this is 'really' funny,
is that the Threadman, Larry, has never been
able to satisfy me. But then again, neither has
Greg," she added as a quick addendum. "He
doesn't have a clue as to what a woman's sexual
needs are. But then again neither does Greg,"
she added as another quick amendment. "As a
matter-of-fact, after the first couple of times
of having experienced substantial nausea from
my relationship with Larry, I wanted out, but
he was holding me emotional hostage. Finally
I got tired of all the pressure and threat of ex-
posure so here we are today."

"So then what you're telling me, Karen,
is that the Threadman became the Threatman."

"You're getting it Pastor Coates."

"I see, but what about the cowboy he
mentioned?"

"Just a nice guy I met at work from somewhere out west. He's here for the rodeo at
Madison Square Garden. I used him to get the
Threadman off my back, literally and figura-
tively. I pretended I was having an affair with
Cody, that's his name, so I'd be cut some
slack."

"Adultery is still pretty serious business
for the life of the soul," her pastor said cautiously.

"Please don't take this disrespectfully
Pastor Coates, but for the past five or so years
Greg and I have lived alone together. My cheating was not a desire for revenge for my unful-
fillment. It was because doors were being
closed on my happiness and late at night a big
old house can get lonely. I can't believe that
God would give us certain feelings and then say,
'Forget them and get into the 'blah'.' Lately I
had been suffering with an excess of real life
'blah' and all I really wanted was to find some
kind of equilibrium, some way to balance it
with a little happiness and pleasantness."

Pastor Coates listened and he never would
have suspected that such a little wish, a single
thing like wanting a little happiness could para-
lyze as good a Christian family as Karen and
Greg Woodward.

"I don't know what encouragement I can
offer you, Karen, You certainly have to decide
what's best for you and Sarah and Teresa." He
knew he should be attempting to save this
woman's marriage; that was what the church
would have wanted. However, still feeling what
he felt in his own soul, he could offer nothing
but his prayers. There was no other course for
him, for her it remained to be seen.

For whatever reason, probably because
she didn't want to admit it to her pastor, Karen

chose not to mention the cruelty Greg had in-
flicted on her in the past. She knew when she
married him that she wasn't really in love with
him, but she was young and pregnant. And
those two qualities certainly had weighed
heavily on everything. She was the kind of
woman not accustomed to flinching. She always played the cards dealt to her, even when
they came from the bottom of the deck.

"I am thankful for your concern and effort, Pastor Coates," she said, her voice small
but earnest.

They got up and walked out of the room.
Out beyond the barn Gregory and the
Threadman were inside the fence looking at the
cows.

Seeing his wife and pastor coming out of
the house, Gregory followed by the Threadman,
met them on the porch.

"Well?" Gregory asked.

Pastor Coates and Karen looked at him.

"Listen, I just had a long talk with Larry
and he assured me, Karen, that your little ad-
venture of the past few months was initiated
by you. It was all your idea."

Karen looked hard at the Threadman.

"He told you that?" she said finally.

"I told Greg about tennis, about the dinners, everything, Karen; I had to."

"That doesn't make it sound so bad then does it Larry? I mean you let me play tennis on your courts and you took me to dinner, and then every once in a while you gave me a fuck. That sounds pretty fair to me. How about you Greg? Is that a good trade off?" Then she started laughing.

"You're crazy, Karen," her husband said.

She was looking down at the Threadman's shoes. His once highly polished Bostonian wingtips were covered with cow dung. She was laughing hysterically. She knew it was going to get even worse. She couldn't help it.

"Get under control," Gregory admonished her.

"Look at your feet, Larry. It's kind of ironic after all the shit you've put me through today. Don't you think?"

Even Pastor Coates had a difficult time restraining himself, her laughter was so infectious.

"Did Larry have a tough time maneuvering through the manure?" she blurted out through a laughing spell.

"I'm glad I can amuse you, Karen," the Threadman replied.

"Greg, I'll bet you don't even know what Larry's favorite dessert is - cowpies."

"That's enough, Karen," her husband said sternly.

"Oh come on Greg, this is the part of the story where the plop thickens," Karen continued.

The Threadman had had enough. He had bared his soul to the pastor and Greg and covered his sole for Karen.

"I'm out of here, Greg. I'll talk to you later. See you Pastor Coates," Larry said turning to leave.

"Hey, want to hit some balls tomorrow?" Greg called out.

"Aren't you teaching?"

"Columbus Day - no school."

"One o'clock?"

"I'll bring the beer."

"This is unbelievable. I can't believe this!" she said. "A neighbor, a member of the same church has been screwing your wife and you act as if he's done nothing."

"He confessed his sin and I respect him for that. Besides, it's more than I heard from you," her husband answered sharply.

Pastor Coates was aware of the volatility

and he deliberately stepped between the couple.

"You are not the first couple, nor will you be the last couple, to have trouble in your marriage," he said, "What you should do is try to understand what has happened, why it has happened and what you can do to work things through." He paused and looked at them for a moment. "I strongly believe that you each know what you must do to live your lives in peace and harmony."

"Peace and harmony!" Greg said curtly. "What about loyalty and obedience?"

"How about honor and love?" Karen exclaimed.

"I'd prefer a little contrition."

"Well I'd prefer a little understanding," Karen retorted.

"You want a little understanding Karen? Well I have a lot of understanding. I understand how you've been lying to me and sleeping with one of my best friends. How's that for understanding?" he shouted at her.

"Lower your voice!" she yelled back out of frustration. "I don't think the neighbors need to hear about our problems," she said under control again. "Perhaps it would be better if you both went inside. I agree that this isn't the best place to discuss this," Pastor Coates explained.

"You're right Pastor Coates, a hundred percent right and I apologize for what you just witnessed. My behavior was unconscionable."

"I know you are both upset, but I think trying to get some positive dialogue going will be beneficial. I'm sure it might alleviate some of the tension between everyone," he said.

"You're right, Pastor Coates," Greg replied. "Maybe it's something I should have done a few months ago."

Karen looked at her husband. She listened to his lies. She knew how she had tried on several occasions to talk with her husband in the past, but he had lost all interest in her needs or happiness, or her daughters' for that matter. His idea of a household in harmony was one with a tyrannical husband to whom everyone else was subservient.

"Why don't I check in on you again tomorrow evening?" Pastor Coates said as he walked back along the path towards his car.

The car hadn't left the driveway when Gregory, entering the dining room behind his wife turned her and struck her across the left eye and side of her face. It was an open handed slap and it sent her reeling against the dining room table.

"I wouldn't let a dog treat me the way you treated me today, Karen," he bellowed at her.

He approached her and grabbed her by the hair and pulled her face to within an inch of his own. She could smell his hot breath on her face.

"I won't have a whore for a wife," he growled, yanking her head back by the hair. "You've humiliated me! How dare you!"

She tried tilting her face away from his, but she could still see the rage in his eyes.

Although he had never struck her before, he had on many occasions been infuriated by even the smallest acts he thought were discordant. He screamed at her as often as he spoke to her. He threw things against the walls or floor when he became outraged; he retaliated with dourness to her attempts at conciliation.

"Who is this cowboy?" he demanded.

"Nobody," she winced. "I just told Larry that so he'd leave me alone."

"I don't believe you, Karen. Why should I believe you?"

"Because it's the truth."

"Here's the truth, Karen," he said maliciously. "This belongs to me." He grabbed her left breast with his free hand while still holding her by the hair with the other. "I own it. Do you understand?"

"You're hurting me, Greg," she cried.

He squeezed her hard then he released her breast and grabbed her between the legs. "This is mine, Karen, when I want it, where I want it, anytime I want it! Get the picture?"

"Stop it!"

"And if I don't want it, it's still mine." He applied pressure there and it hurt her greatly. "Mine, not some cowboy's, not somebody you've met along the way, or had a drink with after work at Morgan's."

She was afraid to move, his grip was so tight. All she wanted was to get through the horrible degradation and get away from him.

"You are nothing more than chattel to me. I own you and will do with you whatever I like. Don't let there be any mistake about it, Karen, none whatsoever."

With that he released his hand and then quickly drew it back and slapped her open-handed between the legs. Karen cried out in pain.

"I'm certainly glad to see you looking more cheerful," he grinned, knowing he had hurt her. "I'm going to make you pay big time for what you've done to me, Karen. I'm going to make you into a nice, straight, simple, good bitch that a husband can be proud of."

With the memory still sharp, of his recent slaps, she knew the fury that preyed upon him had only one outlet. She knew he would be true to his word and would take delight and satisfaction in her suffering. She considered the situation very deliberately and concluded that it would be in her best interest to refuse to struggle. Her husband loved competition and he would have been thrilled to have her resist.

"Every time and anytime I feel like it I'm going to remind you of your terrible error of judgment," he said. "I'm going to refresh your memory as to my feelings about disloyalty."

Karen knew the words he was waiting for, but she couldn't say them. She knew, "I'm sorry," would have been a start, but now it had become a test for her, seeing how much she might put up with until she'd have to give in.

She thought she would like to lie down. Her face and eye stung. She made her way to the sofa and he followed her there.

"Think about something cheerful," she told herself. "Remember something pleasant."

From the way he squinted his eyes she knew he was not finished. "I'll be breathing down your neck, watching you like a hawk from now on," he bristled. "This has been going on for how long, Karen? Months? Years? Anytime my back was turned?"

At that moment she hated the Threadman more than she could have thought possible. She had behaved stupidly by investing in that relationship, by putting her trust in him.

Now she was mired in her own helplessness and it was clear that that fact was very obvious to Greg. She tried to think of anything that would take her mind off of a plan of resistance. She knew he was in control completely and there would be no debate or compromise besides, she had nothing to negotiate with.

She thought about her morning chores, going through that daylight's first hour in her mind, gathering eggs, draining milk from Irene and Isabelle, getting her girls off to school.

Somehow he was able to read her mind. Maybe that's what happens even to people who no longer care about each other, but have been together for so many years.

"I think that the first reward I should give you for polishing your reputation so well is to get rid of the cows. I'm sure having less responsibility outside of our delightful domicile will give you more time to concentrate on me and my needs," he said caustically.

She couldn't help it; his words affected her. She felt the tears welling up inside her. For weeks this man would go without saying more than a handful of words and now very methodically he used them expertly to cut her to the core.

Karen felt herself sinking further into the quagmire of helplessness.

The truth was she was weak. Her future was being laid out for her in her husband's daily planner. She could see the years flipping over, one by one, as his voice droned on.

"You see, my dear, you're going to have to work real hard at restoring your tarnished reputation and I'm going to have a nice list of things for you to do to clean up the embarrassment and disgrace you've put me through," he said standing over her.

Her stomach was churning and she was afraid she might start vomiting, which would have been another disaster. At the same time, unable to control the flow that had been building up, she burst into tears.

"Poor Karen, poor little birdie, has the mean old man made you cry?" he said facetiously. "Am I making you uncomfortable?" he said without blinking his eyes.

Then he reached down and grabbed her by the hair again. "Get used to it!" he said combatively.

She was like a rag doll in his clutches. He was excited by the panic he saw in her eyes.

Jim McBride

"Obviously," her husband said, "there are extraordinary possibilities I could suggest right now to coax along your contrition, but I'll let your imagination take you to what those proposals might be."

He drew a long breath and released her. Then almost abruptly his demeanor changed and he just looked at her confidently knowing any hopes she could ever have of eluding him were non-existent. He became cool and silent and just looked at her in a kind of astonished silence.

Staring at him it pained her and sent a shiver through her body as she remembered the cruelties that had come from his hand and tongue. She knew they were guarantees that would interrupt every minute of her future life and there was no doubt that as long as she stayed in that house he would be able to carry out all that he wished.

Karen knew he would chisel away at her, carve away at her until any physical or emotional strength she might have had would be gone. He would use his words and hands as scalpels and unsympathetically cut her up until she was too weak to resist and then he'd throw her away, like some Thanksgiving Day carcass, into the garbage.

Then like a distracted Hamlet he turned

82

and walked towards the porch, stopping only for a moment to address her once more. "I'll be back at six," he said curtly. "Have dinner ready."

It was as if God were watching over her. She never believed Greg would have let her out of his sight ever again, but for some reason he was leaving the house. She was still frightened. His anger had not lost its force and it made her skin tingle the way the heat of the sun does at the beach.

She waited until his car had disappeared beyond the end of the street before she ran out to gather her children up.

Without explanation or exposition she quickly piled them into her car, announcing only after they were a couple of miles away from home, that they would be staying the night at her mother's house. Karen knew her daughters would be happy to visit with their grandmother because there was no school the next day and there they were always treated like princesses.

Jim McBride

Chapter V

C ody Stewart picked up the phone in his room at the Hotel Earle. He had an awful day in the chutes and the only thing he'd be bringing back to Arizona were some stories about the big city of New York. Then again, he thought, that was okay because that was one of the things he had dreamed about a long time ago when he was a boy - going east to New York to ride in the Square Garden.

The rodeo was over and still his money was not nearly gone. He had made it through the week without experiencing the usual difficulties he had anticipated. The familiar pattern of rodeo life he had known had somehow given him a reprieve and he was happy with life's offered compromise.

He dialed his home number.

"You'd better not think about it," he told

himself, because he knew that as soon as a man got cocky about the way his life was going, his life got complicated. He would get back home, settle in for the winter, and in the spring work as hard as he had ever worked before. He looked forward to getting back to Poorcrow and Tom and the small ranch which provided him with the security to live somewhat as he pleased.

After five rings I, his partner in Window Rock, picked up.

"Hello, Billy. It's me, Cody." Then he added a "Good," responding to a question I had asked about his health and well-being.

"Less than even, but I still have some money left and I met some nice folks."

It was a little while later that I told him how Tom had run off shortly after he left.

"That dumb dog," Cody said. "No sign of him anywhere?" he asked me from the end of the line. "Has he been around for any food?"

Cody knew that his luck had been too good to be true, and sure enough a complication had come up right on schedule.

"Well, I plan to leave here tomorrow afternoon, right after lunch," he told me.

Then not being a fan of telephones, television, computers, or any other of man's technological advances, he ended the phone call rather than get into some kind of perfunctory conversation.

"I'll call you again in the middle of the week," Cody said and hung up.

Sitting on the edge of the sofa he could see that it was beginning to get dark outside. Past the fountain in Washington Square the lights of apartment buildings started popping on, turning the approaching darkness into a muddied shadiness. As he looked up Fifth Avenue it seemed strange that the street with usually the most traffic was now fairly empty. Of course it was a Sunday evening and the weather had turned a bit cooler than it had been. Most of the cafes had pulled in their chairs from the sidewalk to prepare for the coming darkness.

As he stared into the dark outside, he heard some muffled footsteps in the hallway followed by a knock on his door.

"Who is it?" he called out as he crossed to the door.

"Room Service."

The voice was deep and indistinguishable. Looking through the small fisheye lens in the door he saw Karen standing there anticipating it's opening. Instead of letting her in Cody replied, "Broom Service? I don't need any Broom Service, ma'am; the place is pretty clean. Come back in the morning."

"Not 'Broom Service'," the voice on the other side of the door echoed back, "Ruin Service."

"Did you say, 'Gloom Service'?" Cody laughed. "I could use some 'Gloom Service'."

"If you don't open this door, cowboy, it's going to be 'Tomb Service'," she giggled.

Cody, smiling, opened the door and let Karen in. "Ruin Service?" he laughed. Then seeing the discoloration around her eye he said, "Hey, what happened to you?"

"An errant soccer ball," Karen lied. "You know kids, sometimes they don't get the ball to go exactly where they kicked it."

Cody Stewart was the kind of man who usually believed anything anyone told him. It wasn't so much that he was gullible, but rather that he still maintained an old-fashioned innocence. So, Karen's explanation didn't sound so unreasonable.

Karen couldn't say what she wanted to say. She didn't have the right and besides she knew she wouldn't be able to get the words out. It wasn't even like they were old friends. All she knew was that despite knowing she shouldn't be there, she was. Karen knew after she dropped off her daughters at her mom's that she would wind up going into the city to see the cowboy. She liked what he was all about - his kindness especially - and spending some time with him then was just what she needed. She told herself she didn't want to wait until the next day and then regret and find too late, after he was gone, a hundred other questions she would have wanted to ask him.

With her fraudulent life having been discovered that afternoon, she sought a few hours refuge in his honesty.

"Still looking for the moon, cowboy?" she asked him.

"If I say yes are you going to start rhyming words with it?" he asked teasingly. "If so you've already covered 'room', 'broom', 'ruin', 'gloom' and 'tomb'," he said laughing.

"Well, there is a full moon tonight," Karen told him. "And if you want to get a look at it I'll take you down to the Battery."

"The battery?" he said quizzically. "Don't tell me. That's how this city stays lit up all night. There's a giant battery somewhere?"

"No, cowboy. It's just a park on the edge of the water and you can get a good view of a moonrise there."

"I'll tell you what I'm going to do

ma'am," he said exaggerating his best western twang. "I'm going to let you take me to your battery to see the moon over New York City, but only if you let me buy you dinner, nothing fancy mind you, on the way back."

"And where might this dinner be taking place, pilgrim?" she asked imitating his south-western dialect.

"Over at the Dugout on Bleaker Street," he said. "I found it last night. My kind of place: sawdust-covered floors, cheap draft beer, and great burgers."

"No thanks," she said with a false frown. "I'll pass."

Then after letting him hang disappointed for a second or two, she continued, "Just kidding, cowboy. Loosen up. I was joking. It sounds great."

For the first time, during that brief exchange, Karen saw something in the cowboy that she hadn't noticed before. She saw that this athletically hard, solemn man with the light hair and inquiring eyes was really very sensitive; he was more sensitive than she had thought, or he had let on. Karen saw in that moment a hurt when he thought she wasn't interested in having dinner with him. It was almost as if she got a glimpse into a part of him that was complicated and secretive, and also reluctantly vulnerable.

Many people had seen him compete over the years. As faraway faces they had watched him ride and sometimes be thrown from the best bucking stock. But win or lose he always carried himself well, just as any no nonsense cowhand would, with a boyish charm and professional modesty. His friends, who saw him up close, knew he was without meanness, unnecessary toughness or malice even though he had become very guarded and cautious since he'd lost Sara.

It was an agreeable walk to the Battery and as they got closer to the water they were able to see the faraway moon rise before them. Almost as if in a dance or ritual it came across the lapping water, slowly with a sensuous rhythm umbrellaing and illuminating the grass around them.

"Wouldn't it be wonderful if it were true?" she said to him as they walked toward a group of benches which seemed newly varnished in the moonlight.

"What's that?" Cody replied.

"If you could make a wish upon the moon." And then turning to him grinning she added, "And it could come true."

"What would you wish for?"

91

"A Mercedes. A house in the south of France. A Leer Jet. A football team that wins. Maybe a...

"You're not leaving anything out are you? Like a partridge in a pear tree or two turtle doves?"

"No, to be honest, I think I'd just settle for one good night's sleep," she said faintly hopeful.

"How about you, cowboy? What would you wish for?"

"Me, Karen? I kind of have everything I've ever wanted. Almost, anyway. I guess what I would wish for is that all my friends' wishes could come true."

He knew when he said it that it wasn't gospel and that there was a thing or two he really missed. And if he'd been given another chance with a wish on the moon he'd ask for Sara back and maybe a family down the line.

"Are they all like you out there?" she asked him, taking a seat on the arm of a bench.

Cody looked at her not fully understanding how she meant it.

"Well, it depends on if it's a good thing or a bad thing you're asking about."

"Please don't take this the wrong way," she said. "It's just that it is so curious. Here you are, this cowboy who comes to New York from...it might as well be the moon," she said motioning towards the white china disk beyond them. "And you don't have any vanity or conceit. Sincerity and kindness are the two most vital parts of your makeup. You don't have any idea, I'm sure, how foreign that is here in the city. Each day I deal with artifice, with those who have been afflicted sufficiently with cynicism and indifference. It's those people who make me happy to rush home to my girls and my cows because at least I know they are real."

Her voice was soothing like a strain of music and as he listened to her Cody was transported back to Bailey Pond and the sounds and language that were once so familiar to his ear.

"I don't know if I'm any different than the other folks out in Arizona," he said appreciatively. "Or any different than the folks right here for that matter. I think if there is any real difference it's got to do with 'time'."

Walking to the other end of the bench Karen was sitting on, he put his left foot up on it's arm and continued. "My partner Billy Poorcrow's father, Henry, used to be an engineer for the Union Pacific Railroad and everyday he'd make a run out to the local spurline. He'd have that engine opened up pretty good and rain or shine, at the same time each day,

Bobby Brandt's bull would wander out on to the tracks. And each day Henry would see the bull standing there, defiantly, in the middle of the tracks, and each day Henry would stop the train, get down from the engine and lure the bull to the side of the roadbed. Everybody for miles around knew this happened each day, and so on any given day at four o'clock in the afternoon people would come and watch Henry and the bull. Now, you are probably wondering why I'm rattling on about this, but there is a point, believe me. The folks where I come from came out to see Henry lure the bull off the tracks. The people where you come from would come out hoping to see Henry run down the bull."

"You're probably right," Karen said.

"The bottom line is out west folks take pride in stopping for the bull. They have patience; they don't even mind talking to each other. Around here they cut through the bull because 'time' is too precious."

Now Karen understood why her girls felt the way they did about hot fudge sundaes. Cody's pleasantness made her feel comfortable. His words were like the hot chocolate sauce melting the ice cream beneath it. Here was a man whom she enjoyed listening to. He made her feel good with an effortlessness that she would not have believed possible.

Tomorrow afternoon, after lunch, he would leave the hotel and the city and head back to the place and the life he had come from. She would return to her home to nurse her wounds and attempt to hold ground.

She liked looking at him. He was handsome, but not in the soap opera star way. She wanted to capture the way he looked at her; he touched all the worn places that had been misused for so many years.

"You were right," he said. "It is a great place to see the moonrise. I appreciate you bringing me by."

"And I appreciate you sharing it with me. What did you call it before? A horsethief moon?"

"You've got a good memory," Cody said.

He looked at her across the length of the bench. She had lowered her eyes and a soft night wind teased her hair and the moonlight became much brighter around them. He didn't like the bruise around her eye and he felt sorry that it had happened. He knew she was a proud woman, besides being very attractive, and he knew she probably felt a little self-conscious about it, but she never let on.

"One of the most enjoyable things I remember in the moonlight," Cody said, "was watching the mustangs run beyond our valley. It's unbelievable - these wonderful lean horses spilling like a river on fire across the range. They'd come down for water, and wait easy and careful, without moving, and then all of a sudden they would panic and run, leaving their long thin shadows behind them."

"That sounds beautiful," Karen said trying to imagine it.

"Sometimes, when the wind was right you could see them moving away from you, getting smaller and smaller into the distance; but the sounds of their hooves on the hard plain seemed to grow louder."

"I've had the same feelings about my money," Karen jokingly responded. "Only it's my dollars that keep getting smaller while my creditors are the ones getting louder."

"I can relate to that," he said. "I had hoped, a few years ago, that I would be a little further along than I am now, but sometimes the money you're counting on doesn't get counted."

"But you do have your ranch."

"That's true, and I'm hoping that expansion isn't too far off into the future. Right now I have a few head of cattle and I'm optimistic, but there's a lot of nonsense going on with grazing fees and I try hard no to get too disappointed or discouraged about it."

"You certainly don't seem like the type to let anything hold up you plans."

"There are a lot of gambles. It used to be that we were at the mercy of the weather. Now, it's not only the weather, but the government, real estate developers, and the luck of the draw. They've become as unpredictable as the weather."

"Luck of the draw?"

"The stock you ride rodeoing. A while back I had an injury that kept me out of competing for a spell, and I could have used the money."

"What happened?"

"Got stepped on pretty good, messed up a couple of discs," he said remembering.

"Sounds awful."

"Eh," he shrugged his shoulders. "Others have had worse." After a second he added, "I've some friends are kind of just glued together. Bobby Brandt, the old timer I spoke about before..."

"With the bull?"

"Right. Well he has the longest arm muscles you'd ever see, from years and years of riding bulls. He's been under the knife so often he's sometimes mistaken for a fork or

97

spoon."

"Isn't the hurt enough to make you quit?"

"It's something you just do, or I should say you just have to do, until you can't do it anymore. Crazy huh?"

"Oh, I don't think it's crazy to have a passion. And if you are possessed then I must tell you, Mr. Stewart, that you are one of the most charming possessed men I've ever met."

The moon was true and in front of them now casting their shadows and the bench's on a deep slant into the dark behind them.

"Thank you," he said.

Cody knew or thought he knew all there was to know about living without a woman. He'd done all he could to stop thinking about what it would have been like living with someone he loved and that loved him. He had tried very hard to forget those little things Sara did that told him she was happy, and so he was happy. As he thought about it, it came to him again that Sara didn't choose love and neither did he; it was love that chose them. It was the luck of the draw.

"What's the matter?" Karen asked, seeing him lost in his thoughts.

"It's going to sound stupid," he replied.

"Try me."

"It's kind of painful for me, being here."

"Is it something I've said or done?" she interrupted.

"If anything, you're helping me," he continued. "Here I am sitting on a park bench two thousand miles from home, and I'm thinking now of what it was like to be happy, remembering something that was good and times I've enjoyed."

"And that's painful?"

"Of all the things you could wish for and have on a horsethief moon is to know when you were happy, and 'lonely' was a word that described other people."

"At least you've had those times." Karen said quietly. "Who is to say when or how much anyone's entitled to? Where does it say everyone gets the same amount of happiness or sorrow or moonlight?" she said gesturing towards the bright hole in the night sky.

"You're right," Cody said. "But you were wrong before - back at the hotel."

Karen looked at him questioningly.

"It was moon service," he laughed.

He kept his eyes focused on the moon she had motioned to; he was afraid if he looked over at her he might tell her how thankful he was she had been so especially nice to him.

·"Just a harmless night in the park," he told himself trying to ignore the stirring inside him.

Karen was different. She was a woman not afraid to compliment a man, or to accept a compliment from a man. Sitting there in the park with her was restful, even though inside him Cody was struggling with some thoughts beyond his powers. He liked her a lot and he was trying to keep from thinking about those urges he wasn't supposed to be having. He wasn't succeeding. The thoughts were too pleasant to put out of his head; they kept him from starving.

"Hey, wake up cowboy." Karen said deliberately, snapping her fingers in front of his eyes.

"Where have you been?"

Cody came back as the shadowy silhouette of Karen's fingers passed across his face, through the moonlight into the dark expanse of the night. In that fraction of a second before, his heart had been alive with Sara's presence. Bright shards of light broke out of his trunk of memories. A million remembrances flashed through his soul in the sweetness of pictures. He remembered the green and the sparkle in her eyes. He remembered the way her mouth curled up in the corners when she smiled. He remembered her favorite pair of boots, the black "Noconas" that she wore on their first date. He remembered the smell of "Opium", her favorite perfume. He remembered that "Desperado" was her favorite song, and also how she danced with him to it in her father's kitchen. He remembered how happy she was when she gave him the Buck knife with the hoof pick for Christmas. He remembered that Christmas was her favorite time of the year. He remembered how she loved *The Nutcracker* and how if she couldn't be a barrel racer she'd like to be the ballerina in pink. He remembered how she loved oatmeal for breakfast...and lunch...and dinner. He remembered her birthdate - the twenty-fourth of October, one day after his. He remembered her sheepskin coat, her horsehair bracelet and her claddah ring. He remembered her favorite tee-shirt, her favorite ball team - the Astros because they had drafted him out of high school. He remembered the buckle she won in Mesquite, her "O'Farrell" hat just like Lane Frost's, and her turquoise earrings. He remembered that her favorite beer was Guinness and her favorite drink was Bailey's in coffee (no sugar or whipped cream). Her favorite book was *Behind the Chutes* because he was in it. Cody remembered all these things, but most of all he remembered that he was her favorite cowboy, not Donny Gay, not George Strait or any other guys she had met along the way. He remembered how much she had loved him; that was the hardest thing to forget.

"Taking a warm bath in memories," he replied. "Sorry."

The return to reality was not painful, but pleasant, like floating across Bailey Pond on an innertube that last summer.

Karen looked at him congenially, casting about for an effective comment to respond with.

"You don't have to be sorry, cowboy, for anything," she said finally and with a simple sincerity.

Cody felt as if she were reading his heart. He looked at her and saw the clearness in her eyes. And with that look she told him more about herself than if she had spoken a million words.

"I have a funny idea. Actually it's a hypothesis," Karen said as she stood up and smiled. "Why don't we walk back to Bleaker Street and I can tell you about it?"

"A hypothesis?" Cody asked pretending to be as dumb as Clay Ford's Jackass. "It's not some kind of woman thing?"

Karen laughed.

"You have to remember, Karen, that I'm just a poor, simple cowboy who comes from the Arizona - New Mexico state line, and these big words are scary to me."

They jauntily moved along the channel-like streets that ran through buildings housing artists' galleries, bookstores, and N. Y. U. students.

"The last time I heard the word 'hypothesis' I was sitting in Mrs. Lukerson's science class my senior year in high school," Cody told her as they walked along. "She was one of those teachers that had to have everything in her room just so. She even had pieces of tape on the floor where each leg of your desk should be."

"Well, at least you still have some respect for her," Karen replied. "You did call her 'Mrs. Lukerson'."

"We used to call her a lot worse than that, believe me. Her real name was Dianne Lukerson and she weighed 300 pounds if she weighed an ounce. Billy and I would spend our study halls making up jokes about her."

"Like?"

"Like what do you call a 300 pound woman who is sexually attracted to men and women?"

Karen looked at him without having the slightest clue or hope of coming up with an answer.

"Bi-Anne Lukerson."

Karen laughed.

"What can you use to fill in the washout gully behind Billy Brandt's barn?"

"I give up," Karen said.

"Try Anne Lukerson." After a pause he asked her, "What do you call a 300 pound bug with bulging eyes that hangs around garbage cans? Fly Anne Lukerson."

Karen was laughing pretty well by the time they had gotten as far as Houston Street.

"What do you call a 300 pound woman who lives like a combination grizzly bear / mountain man in the Wyoming wilderness?" Cody asked for the last time.

Karen looked at him in amazement..

"Cheyenne Lukerson."

"Sounds to me like you and your friends had a lot of fun back then and it seems like you haven't changed too much since then," Karen said giggling.

"I try." Then Cody added, "Don't get me wrong Karen, I actually did learn a couple of things from Mrs. Lukerson, like, 'two pieces of matter can not take up the same amount of space at the same time.' She used to say that all the time."

Karen and Cody continued their walk towards Bleaker Street. Every now and again he would tip his hat to a woman passing by or acknowledge someone on a corner waiting patiently for a light to change.

"One time Billy brought a polecat, a skunk, into our science class and the first thing Mrs. Lukerson said was, "What about the smell, Billy?"

"That's okay, Mrs. Lukerson," he replied. "He'll get used to you."

Karen laughed at the cowboy whose humor was fast becoming a habit.

"So tell me about your hypothesis, Karen," he said.

"First of all," she said, "I think there is hope for you. Unfortunately, you have been raised in an environment which has lent itself to your delusion. Basically what this means," she said chuckling, "is that you are mentally unstable, unbalanced, living in an abnormal mental state, certifiably (There is no question in my mind.) crazy."

"I see," replied the cowboy.

"Well, I don't really think you see, in the seeing sense of the word, because if you saw what you should see you would have seen that you didn't see what was worth seeing."

Cody looked at her trying to somehow fathom what she was saying with false interest.

"Okay Karen, you'll have to bear with me for just a second and I'm going out on a limb right now," he said laughing pretty hard. "And I hope I'm not making a big mistake, but - I hear what you're saying."

This was just what Karen needed: more ammunition, more fodder.

"Cody," she said, "sometimes it is hard to hear things that you don't want to hear because hearing them reminds you of things you may have at one time heard before. Do you see what I mean?"

Karen was smiling and laughing, having fun with the word play going on between them.

"Okay, will you hear what I say when I say I saw something which can only be heard by people who've seen it before?" she asked him.

"Yes."

"You poor misfortunate cowboy, think that living free, punching cows, beating up calves, socking heifers, and castrating bulls under the wide open sky is the way to live. But, my new friend, you are wrong. If God had meant men and women to live like that he would not have created cities, tenement buildings or subways. Of course not. Your problem is that you haven't been brought into the Twentieth Century yet. Evolution wise, you are behind the times, but as I mentioned before - there is hope. Here is my hypothesis: If you stay in New York for thirty days or so, then I guarantee that I can bring you up to speed. You can become a Twentieth Century cosmopolitan urban dweller. I can drain that provincialism right out of you."

"And how would you do that?" he said trying to control himself, cross the street, laugh, and hold his side simultaneously.

"The first thing I'd do is get rid of that hat, then the boots, and those dungarees."

"And what would you replace them with?"

"Who said anything about replacing them? I just said we'd get rid of them." Cody looked at her for a long second as they reached the steps of The Dugout. "You, yourself, said only a little while ago to 'bare with you'."

"I thought I meant 'bear with me'," he said as they made their way into what was once the basement of an old apartment building.

"I am starting to get a whole new understanding of what city people are like," he said as they got themselves a table in the corner away from the door.

"Understanding," she said, "a noun, could be used as an adjective."

"Understanding." Cody repeated, then after a moment he said, "You're a pretty bright and quick woman, Karen. I can (He raised his fingers into quotation marks.) understand that."

"My husband teaches grammar, remember?"

"That's right, but still there's more to it than that. Right?"

"I put in a couple of years of college, but with a baby and stuff early on, things got a little derailed."

"I understand, seriously," he added.

"You're understanding." she laughed.

The waitress came over to take their orders and Cody told her that "Understanding" was the word for the night; it could be used either as a noun or as an adjective. Both would be perfectly acceptable.

"Do you drink suds?" Cody asked.

"Suds?"

"Beer?"

"My father spent most of his life working for the Turnpike Authority, and my three brothers went to every home game that the Mets played when I was a kid. And you ask me if I drink beer?"

"Put that gun down, Missy; I'll go peaceably."

Then turning to the waitress he said, "Give Belle Star here anything she wants, ma'am, and I'll have a Coors draft."

"Do you have Guinness?" Karen asked.

"Only in bottles," the waitress replied.

"That's fine."

"Guinness?" Cody inquired smiling again.

"My father's name was Patrick Brennan and my brothers are Pat, Tommy and Kevin. My family is as Irish as the Pope is Catholic and you are surprised that I like Guinness?"

"Well then, we must be related," he said.

"How is that?" Karen asked.

"Because my family is as Scottish as the day is long. Besides, everyone knows a Scotsman is just an Irishman with shoes."

"I thought it was an Irishman wearing a skirt," she laughed.

"No, sorry. That's not true. Did you ever try to strap on chaps over a kilt and ride through mesquite and prickly pear? It's not much fun," he replied amiably.

"I'll bet," Karen returned as they both laughed together.

Then impulsively she reached across the table and took hold of his hand.

"Thank you for making me laugh tonight," she said quietly. "I needed it."

As quickly as she had taken his hand she released it.

"Sure, anytime," Cody said almost in a whisper.

The waitress brought them their drinks and took their order for two burgers and a basket of fries.

"Over the river and through the woods," he said lifting his glass towards her. Karen raised her bottle and clinked it against his glass.

"That's a strange toast," she said.

"It's a habit from a few years back."

"Am I being intrusive if I ask what it means?"

"Sara had this great simplicity of wisdom. She never stopped astonishing me," he said. "Whenever we were having a drink she would raise her glass and list all of the great places and things we'd done together that made us happy. After a while the list just got bigger and bigger and it took longer to say the toast than it did to drink the beer. So one day she cut it down to, 'Over the river and through the woods,' knowing that both of us knew what it meant."

A smile played across Karen's face. "She must have been very romantic," she said in a friendly voice.

"She was," he said thinking to himself how she was also charming and pleasant and beautiful.

"I'm sorry for your loss," Karen said sincerely.

Cody nodded his thanks and then added, "I never thought life could be so humbling."

"I never thought it could turn so sour,"

"What do you mean?"

"Sometimes there are things that happen that you never want another soul in the world to know."

Cody looked at her without understanding.

"I'm sorry," she said seeing his confusion. "I don't mean to wish my problems on you."

"There are a lot of folks whose problems I wouldn't care to hear about, but you're not one of them Karen," he said assuringly.

"I guess it's just that I don't have anyone else to talk to and once again, cowboy, you're sitting in the lucky seat."

"It's okay. There's no cost," Cody said.

Like water running underground, very slowly Karen let herself go. She brought to the surface her troubles and pain and the fears which she had held suspended in mid-motion since the afternoon. Then with shaky resolve she began.

"I hope you don't think me foolish or crazy. And I certainly know I haven't any right to even tell you any of this, but for some reason I have to. Maybe it's just because you know how to love and be loved and I've forgotten."

Cody looked at her transfixed.

"I'm jealous," she said. "But don't take it the wrong way. I'm jealous of the fact that you are able to still love and care about your Sara. And believe me, I don't mean that to be cruel. I'm jealous of the fact that two people could love that way."

Cody studied her face. It was the face of a beautiful woman who was once at peace, but was now losing her remaining hope.

"I lied before when I said I broke off my relationship with the Threadman because I wanted to work on my marriage. I ended it for many reasons, but most importantly because I was afraid of Greg and what he'd do if he found out. Since the end of the summer he'd been getting harder and harder to live with and I could see a kind of cruelty seeping into him that was never there before.

"You've been around some awful people it seems," Cody said.

"Awful I could handle. It's when awful turns into mean and nasty that I get afraid."

She looked at the cowboy imploringly, hoping that he would understand how everything had become so disappointing and difficult.

"Today the Threadman came to my home to confess his sins to my husband. He brought our pastor along with him. He told Greg everything that was going on, even mentioning how you were the new love of my life."

"And I thought we only had hangings out in the old west," Cody said trying to bring a little humor to the seriousness of the situation. Then he continued, "It must have been a real lousy party."

"I used to pride myself on the fact that there was a lot of stuff I could take, that I could put up with. I thought I was tough as nails; but I was wrong."

"Boy, that's real brave of them. Three grown men ganging up on a little girl. What

113

did they do, let the pastor hold you while they took their best shots at you? What did your husband say to Saint Threadman?"

"He said he'd play tennis with him to-morrow afternoon."

"What?"

"Greg was pleased that Larry confessed. He doesn't have any problem with him. It's me."

"I'll bet when they're not playing tennis they're walking on water." Cody said.

The waitress brought them their burgers and as they ate the conversation continued.

"You know what I like about you, cow-boy?"

"My hat?" Cody interjected.

"I like that too. It's kind of neat and so are your boots."

"Tony Lamas," the cowboy explained.

"They make boots out of llamas?"

"No, it's a man's name."

"Oh, well anyway, as I was saying, what I like about you is the glimpse you've given me. It's a glimpse of something that was once familiar and wonderful and worth remember-ing."

Karen looked at him and she knew he was

like the candle flame set in glass upon their table. He was making clear to her what she knew already, but had clouded in dimness for such a long time. "The future would always be like that dimness if she kept living in the past," she thought looking into his eyes shining in the candle's glow.

For Karen The Dugout was a gentle place, an oasis which claimed her and took her away from the panic that had flooded her earlier in the day.

Cody's face and eyes had their own language and it told her something which could not be said with words. He helped her to break out of the boundaries of the here and now. She knew life with her husband would be impossible from now on. She just wasn't sure if she was strong enough to survive.

"You can talk about it, you know, if you want to," Cody said.

"I suppose we all learn from our mistakes," she said. "I just kind of made the worst ones."

"I wouldn't be so hard on myself if I were you."

"It's going to make things pretty complicated, and I don't have any answers," she said. "I wish I could say, 'I'll work things out,' but I don't want to. God I hope my girls don't think

I'm the stupidest mother in the world."

"You haven't been stupid, from what I can see, from where I sit in the lucky seat," hc replied.

"You're kind," she said with a voice that could break your heart.

This time Cody stretched his hand across the table and gently touched her face.

"This is ridiculous," she said. "Here I am spilling my insides to some cowboy I met two days ago who traveled 2,000 miles across the country to see New York, not to listen to confessions."

"Some cowboy?" Cody asked. "How many times do I have to tell you about the luck of the draw?" He paused for a moment and looked into her eyes. "Now this is probably the corniest thing you'll ever hear, but it's kind of true. In, rodeo you hope and pray to draw the rankest of the rough stock..."

"Stop there," Karen interrupted. "I'm lost already. What is 'rankest'?"

"Meanest."

"Why do you want the meanest?"

"Because the judges score you and the horse you've drawn. So, if you draw some wall-eyed old plow-horse who doesn't try to kill you, no matter how well you ride, you're not going to score very high."

Karen was caught up for the moment in his voice and the pleasantness of his face. He was still tanned from the summer and the white around his eyes made them seem even bluer than before.

"Now here comes the wisdom of the ages, missy," he said laughing at himself, bringing her back to him. "The part that's corny, so don't fall asleep on me."

Karen came back. She liked the way he had become animated and excited about the life he was leading.

"The key is balance. You have to sit in the middle and keep your free hand free. You can hold on to the rein or rigging with one hand - just like you can hold on to family or friends or loved ones, but you still have to remember to keep one hand free. And it's always seemed to me that this is what life is about. You shouldn't hold on to anything with both hands; you shouldn't have a fear of having some freedom. Everyone must find the right balance."

Karen listened silently following the words.

"Don't get me wrong, Karen, I believe as much as anyone that you should hold on to those you love as tightly as you can. Just like holding on to a bareback rigging, your five fingers know how the hand aches. Well, so does

117

the soul that once held a heart so close."

"You're a lucky fellow, Cody Stewart," she said looking into the cheerful face and kind eyes beneath his chocolate-colored Resistol.

"You see, Karen, the tougher the ride life gives you, the higher the score you'll get."

Karen bit her lip and looked away. Then she reached up and touched the bruise along the side of her face.

"The truth is that this wasn't really caused by a miskicked soccer ball," she said in almost a hushed whisper. Unexpectedly her face turned white and a couple of tears slipped from her eyes.

"Are you all right?"

"Greg used a tried-and-true method to keep my attention - his hand," she said closing her eyes.

"Tennis balls weren't available?" Cody said, his voice intense and gnawing. "He must be a real decent human being. Real decent."

"He's always had this thing about author-ity."

"That's not about authority, Karen, that's about meanness."

"I guess, according to your theory then, I'm going to get a pretty high score," she replied trying to regain a little composure.

"Let me explain something to you," he said very troubled by what had happened to her. "I've seen cruelty before and I know that it's something that doesn't go away by wishing it away. It's something that works its way steadily further into the bones, and once an animal or a man has it within him it only will get worse."

Cody eased a little closer to her across the table. "I wish the world around you wasn't the way it is," he said with a sincere kindness trying to ease the tension that had a grip on her.

"How is he with your daughters?"

"They're afraid of him so they are pretty cautious not to get him upset. I've become sort of the cushion between them and Greg."

Cody shook his head. He took a swallow of the beer and felt the cold of the frosted glass against his palms.

"Sometimes it's almost funny the way the girls maneuver and tip toe around the house trying to avoid being in the same room with their father," Karen told him.

"Sounds pretty scary to me."

"It's a long way from being just scary," Karen said.

"A rope, no matter how strong, can be pulled so taut," Cody offered, putting his glass

119

back on the table next to the candle jar.

"He'd always make some remark about the way the girls were dressed or how they fixed their hair. And for kids so young, that kind of criticism can be too much."

"That sure sounds like a good way to live, playing hide and go seek with your father." Then Cody asked, "Where are they now?"

"I dropped them off at my mom's for the evening. Since there's no school tomorrow they'll get in a good visit with grandma."

"Just a little detour around a dangerous curve?" the cowboy asked.

"When you're the escaping prisoner you do whatever you have to do to gain some time." Karen offered matter-of-factly. "I'm not going to spend the rest of my life guarded by a sentry called 'husband'. And I'm not going to have my family bound in by ten foot high emotional barbed wire fencing."

"Are you sure that's what you want?"

"You know, cowboy, as I was driving here this afternoon I thought about what kind of life I've had, particularly the last two or three years. And I came to realize that anything would be better than the precautions and games I've been forced into by Greg. Anything would be better than the rigidness and vindictiveness my life has been wrapped in. Hopefully," she added, "I'll find some comfortableness some place, some where." She looked at him hoping he would understand.

"It's kind of now or never. Greg went off for a while, probably to get a bottle of wine, and instead of preparing his dinner I prepared our escape."

"Good for you."

"It was an easy decision, really. Believe me. Today was just the culmination. When I think about some of the things he's done to me I wonder why I've waited this long."

Cody knew why. This woman, it was obvious, loved her daughters. He knew there was nothing false about her. When it came down to putting their welfare on the line she had to do what she had to do.

"One time last summer we were running along the shore and I got a stitch in my side and had to stop. Greg wanted to keep going and when I told him I had to wait he dragged me into the water and held me under."

"Was he just fooling around? Kidding?"

"No, he was upset that I couldn't keep going. That's the way he is."

Their waitress brought them another round of drinks and as "Time" harnessed the hour Karen spoke more of what her husband had put them through.

"I was frying some chicken for dinner and doing a couple of hundred other things simultaneously, when without thinking I splashed some hot oil on my hand. It blistered up pretty good and hurt for over a week, making dishwashing and other tasks difficult. Needless-to-say, Greg thought I was milking it, trying to get out of doing my usual chores."

"He really expected you to carry on with your normal routine with your hand the way it was?"

"He said it would make a man out of me."

"Maybe that's what he's wanted all along. Maybe he should have been the one having the affair with the Threadman. Now that would have been a fun thing for your pastor to sort out."

Cody smiled an irregular smile and as he did Karen chuckled to herself picturing her husband and the Threadman discussing their homosexual affair in a casual manner with Pastor Coates.

"Another time, and this sort of thing happened a lot, he was supposed to pick up Sara at home after work and bring her to her team's soccer game. But when he got home he said he was too tired and the poor kid wound up running the three miles to the school field while he laid down."

"You know what I would like, Karen?" Cody said looking into her eyes from beneath his hat. "I'd like to meet your husband in a phonebooth with just enough space for us to have a pleasant little conversation."

"Believe me, I wish I could arrange it," she replied. Then after a few moments she said, "A couple of months ago I woke up feeling that I had been unconscious for years. I had come to the realization that my life was running along without me. I was married to a man who ignored me and who had basically unloaded me. I knew that the Threadman was lonely and I knew he would not be reluctant to get involved with me, even though Greg was his friend. He had made overtures to me in the past."

Cody listened.

"I guess the loneliness had just built up for so long that I didn't care about the risk. I didn't care what I would say to Greg when and if I got caught. All I wanted was someone to hold me and want me. Little did I know, as smart as I thought I was, that weasels could take on human form."

Cody smiled.

"You know what's almost hysterical? It's that he couldn't even satisfy me and still, even with that realization, I continued to sleep with him. It wasn't even love making, but at any rate, I wasn't strong enough to end it sooner because as bad as it was, I needed it."

For Cody it was as if she had struck a match in a dark corridor and was asking him to follow her through. As long as he listened she would be all right. She needed him to believe in her, to trust her and not look at her as a woman intent on madness.

He followed her, pausing with her at various memories that hemmed her in. She held the match under each one, illuminating the difficult stops along her life. Fascinated, Cody listened as her experiences surfaced and then vanished into the night leaving behind the awfullest taste in his mouth.

"I'll say one thing for you, Karen, you're not a quitter. A lot would have pulled in their ropes long before now."

"Some place inside I was silly enough to believe I could make it work. For a long time I ignored what Greg was doing to us. I felt it was my fault the marriage was falling apart. No matter what I tried I couldn't get it to work," she said earnestly.

"You don't have to apologize for yourself," Cody replied. "You certainly have earned your wages."

As Karen smiled at him he could sense an innocence and girlishness that she still possessed. There was a purity about it and he did not doubt for a moment that what was happening there in The Dugout between them was not dangerous. He had noticed in her, when she was waiting on him at Morgan's that there was something unusual and extraordinary in her.

Maybe it was the beer or the conversation or the fact that in a very vague way The Dugout reminded him of The Doghouse where he and Sara and their friends had had so many happy times together.

He even thought yesterday when he first discovered it, hidden deep on Bleeker Street, how the bartender reminded him of Fred the owner of The Doghouse.

"If you ever get out my way, to Arizona, I'll take you to a place that's very similar to this," he said saying it almost like a vow.

"I'd like that."

"You would, believe me. You'd like The Doghouse and I know you'd fit right in."

"That's a very strange name for a place to eat; don't you think?"

"Not really. It was first called Fred and Rose's, but pretty soon so many cowhands were stopping by with their cowdogs trailing behind them, that the name just kind of took on itself. Believe me, it wasn't unusual to have five or six of them lying under the pool tables. Cowdogs that is."

"Isn't that sort of against the local Board of Health's regulations?" Karen asked.

"Heck, Fred was the Board of Health, and the Building Inspector and the Postmaster and just about everything else on God's green earth."

Secretly, during that moment, Karen crossed her heart and promised herself that one day she would travel west to that strangely named curiosity called The Doghouse.

"Will you excuse me for a minute?" she said. "I should call my mom and make sure Teresa and Sarah are okay."

"Sure."

He watched in the mirror as she walked across the sawdust-covered floor past the flickering flames of the candle jars. He sat there incredulous, feeling helplessly overpowered by what had been taking place all evening. He knew if any of his old friends had been there they would have seen it too: how much she was like Sara. As the evening had progressed he'd seen how more and more in each and every way Karen reminded him how difficult it had been to live the last years without Sara.

126

Cody remembered the way Sara's room looked the day after her funeral: just like she would be back any minute. Her Fedco Seeds catalog, with the half-filled order form, was sitting on the night stand next to her bed. Her favorite book, *The Miracle Worker*, was lying on an old oak chest next to some newly washed boot socks. The latest copy of *The Cowboy Gazette* was tucked between the lamp and the telephone with an ad for a porcupine quill hat band circled in red.

Karen wove her way back to him through the sociable world of The Dugout crowd.

"Everything all right?" he asked her as she sat down.

"As good as could be expected." Then she added, "Greg called my mother when we weren't home for dinner and told her that since he'd be playing tennis in Belleport tomorrow afternoon he'd pick up the girls around four."

"Did he say anything to your mother about...?"

"No, just business as usual as far as he's concerned."

"I don't imagine the way he behaved is something he'd want to brag to anyone about, especially your mom."

"Nobody in his right mind might not say

127

anything, but you've got to remember we're talking about Greg. Then again, he's probably as happy as can be with the whole household gone. I'm sure he's figuring out the rule changes he thinks I'm going to be living by from now on."

"What will you do about all that?"

"I'm not sitting here blindfolded. I can see what the future holds," she said seriously. "And I'm certainly not foolish enough to put my hands in boiling water."

Then an unimpaired grin broke out across her face and she said, "Maybe I'll go on a cruise, or sign up for the next moon shot, or perhaps take the girls to the Bahamas and set up a lemonade stand."

"At least you still have your sense of humor."

"That's probably all I'll have after this mess is cleared up."

"Remember what I told you about a list," he said trying to offer some kind of encouragement.

"The only list I want to make out is a 'party' list. Maybe I should just schedule a gigantic 'bash' - a separation party - a you go your way, I'll go mine extravaganza. I could have all my friends; you'd be invited too, cowboy, and Greg could have his. Oh, I forgot, he only has one - Saint Larry the Confessor."

"Do you really like parties?" Cody asked.

"I used to."

"So did Sara."

Cody looked at her and he remembered Sara's last birthday like it was yesterday. It was a small gathering of friends and some family members. And when it was over she asked him to give her a ride out to see her grandmother at the nursing home. It was the first birthday Dolly, her granny, was unable to attend and Sara wanted to bring her a piece of cake. He dropped her off at the entrance while he went to park his truck. When he came back and went into the room he found Sara lying on the bed with her grandmother, holding her and telling her how much she loved her and missed not having her at her party. It was a very beautiful thing to see.

"Well, here's to our own little party right here," Karen said raising her drink.

She did it as though she were saying, "You and I are friends now. And even if sometimes life can get painful we can fight off the madness with laughter."

"Today with Greg and Pastor Coates, for the first time in my life, I felt like an alien and that I was being banished like a child from the company of adults." Karen said. "Even though I knew what I had done was wrong in their eyes I still had a great belief in God and a great faith. Maybe it was naive to think that no matter what I did in life I would always, somehow, be protected and I trusted that I would always be kept safe," She paused for a moment. "until Greg hurt me today. In just a few short minutes of a lifetime he contaminated what I felt was a birthright."

Cody listened as Karen spoke of her torment earlier that day.

"As bad as it was it brought about a realization for me. I'll make the decision about what I will or will not do now, and more importantly what I'll let anyone else do to me. If any good has come from all of this it's that it's made me stronger, given me a real strength because I know it means that only I am responsible for my own happiness."

Karen looked away from him. It was longer than usual before she looked back at him.

He knew she was going to be all right. She was like the young cottonwood, where the riverbank turned upstream and flowed into Bailey Pond. When other trees would give up and die away with nature's unpredictability the cottonwood survived. Each spring its roots went deeper and held together the soil at the very spot where Cody and Sara used to sit and talk about the future.

"A hop, a skip, a jump here and there and things have a way of getting back on track," the cowboy said.

"You're right," Karen returned. "Who knows, maybe someday I'll be on the Union Pacific running on those tracks west. And perhaps we will become two great friends who never see each other except to wave through the window of a passenger train."

"I hope not," Cody replied. "Not the business of becoming great friends, but the never seeing each other again part."

She looked at him, her face framed by the wheat-colored hair that smokily fell to her shoulders. Her eyes sparkled even in the dimness of the room and her skin glowed fair and smooth.

"It is very strange how things work out," he began. "Today has been a very difficult and unpleasant day for you."

"Really, Karen interjected smiling, "I hadn't noticed."

"Anyway, you've had your world turned upside-down, but for me, and I mean no disregard or disrespect, it has been one of my happiest in a long time. I've found, as you've said, a new friend and the irony of all this is that if you did not have such an awful day I, most likely, would not be having a happy one. Pretty bizarre, isn't it?"

"Whoever would have 'thunk it', cowboy," she said smiling. "I'm glad somebody has had a good day and really this last part hasn't been too bad for me either."

"Not too bad?" he said warmed by her comment and smile. "You wouldn't have even gotten a bite out of that burger if you were out with the power eater tonight," he laughed.

"What can I say? As a friend of mine has said, 'It's the luck of the draw'," she replied watching his melancholy eyes narrow as he grinned.

Her voice was pleasantly warm.

"Thank you," he said.

"For what?"

"For letting me feel that I'm still kind of human. It's like finding an unredeemed voucher in your pocket that you didn't know you still had."

"Neglect will do that."

"I know," he said. "That's one of the other things I've done, almost as good as polite." He paused for a moment and then continued. "After the accident I wasn't too good for much and I figured the best way to deal with Sara's death was to get off by myself for some solitude. So just like Gene or Roy at the end of the movie, the cowboy rode away, right into the setting sun. I swear I could almost hear the 'Sons of the Pioneers' singing off in the distance."

Karen looked at him, intrigued with his candor. He was opening up and she was happy that he felt comfortable enough to share some of what he'd been through.

"I took my dog, Tom, and we rode up to an old line shack that runs out a lot of miles from Billy Brandt's. We stayed there for quite a while, just the two of us having these great conversations. I'd rattle on for days and old Tom, he'd just wag his tail and nod his head. I think he knew the madness was approaching and he didn't want to become masterless so he did everything to aggravate me. He'd jump on me, pull on my pants, step on the heels of my boots when I walked around, and nip at my shirt when I sat looking at the fire. He did everything to keep me from having too much time to feel sorry for myself."

"Sounds like a pretty good friend to have around," Karen said.

"He was and it was his being such a pest

that helped get me through. I must have opened and closed the door to that cabin a hundred times a day, day after day. Let him out; let him in; let him out; let him in. It's true what they say, 'The dog trains his master'."

"I give you this cowboy, not too many people take having a 'little hair of the dog...' as seriously as you."

Cody laughed.

"Yeah, I've kind of always taken everything literally."

"And that's part of your charm. No fault, no blame."

The voice of his heart told him to tell her the rest.

"Day and night there was this little creature living inside me trying to carve me up and eat away at me. And dumb me, I didn't know how or really care how to get rid of him. But Tom, he knew; and over and over with renewed effort he made me open that door and close that door. I swear, I was about to scream when it finally came to me. The door was the key. When a door opens, someone either comes inside or goes outside. The door was there and I just had to decide which side I wanted to be on."

"Seems like that cowdog of yours was

134

pretty smart and pretty protective."

"Yeah, I'm going to miss him."

"Maybe he'll be back when you get home."

"I don't know; usually when they run off it's forever."

Karen listened with almost a slight envy to the way Cody spoke about the friendship he's had for Tom.

"Early one morning, while the sky was still muddied, we closed the door behind us for the last time," he continued. "Eventually, I started to make the rounds again; the most frequent stop being The Doghouse. I nearly drove Fred and Rose and their customers crazy for a month or so. I played the same George Strait song on the Jukebox over and over. I put enough money in that machine to own it. It got so that when they saw my pickup pull into the yard somebody went over and pulled out the plug."

"I had just about used up all my chances when my pulse began beating again and the long suffering started to ease up. I was lucky to have around me some friends who could not only see when someone was banged-up or crippled in a corral and understand their hurt, but could also see the more difficult - the invisible - when a heart had been mangled."

135

Then grinning again he added comically, "And I did it without feathers too."

"What do you mean?"

"The 'homing instinct'. Like a pigeon, I came back to the familiar. Of course if I were a pigeon I would have come back in Tom's mouth."

Cody Stewart had taken the time to study what had happened to him. He knew what it was to live through loss and what happened to the people who had been through it. He also knew that he was a survivor and in the future nothing could ever be so bad that he couldn't get through it.

Even though he was in his twenties when Sara died, Cody was still, at that time, in many ways a boy. But when he came back with Tom from the line shack he had begun to change. It was gradual. He stood straighter and he carried himself like a young John Wayne in *Red River*. He paid attention to details, even the minutest details. He treated people fairly, squarely and he expected to be treated the same.

He had refused to let himself be left high and dry by the receding tide of remorse that had engulfed him. He returned to cowboying and rodeoing and worked steadily at making something that would last.

Their meals were finished and the returning waitress asked if they would like another round.

"None for me," Cody said. Then turning back to Karen he said, "Two's my limit, but you can have whatever you'd like."

"I'm fine too," Karen responded. "Only two beers?" she inquired. "That's another thing I never would have 'thunk' about you."

"Believe me, a few years ago I would have had my share, but time changes a man."

A few minutes later they settled up the bill and made their way up the steps and out of The Dugout on to Bleeker Street.

"I'm not going to walk you back to your car," Cody said mildly as they passed under the marquee of The Circle In The Square Theatre. Then before she could say anything or register a reaction he said, "I know I don't have any right to interfere in your life, Karen, but I think it might be a little rough for you back home tonight, so if you don't mind staying at The Earle at least I'll know you'll be all right."

It had been a while since a man had shown a genuine interest in her well-being and for the slightest moment Karen was overcome. It was an experience she had forgotten about - being cared about rather than being the carer. Still recovering and catching her breath she said, "You don't have to do that, cowboy. I can stay at my Mom's with the girls."

"I'd appreciate it if you'd indulge me," Cody replied. "I don't have any sinister plans. I'll even let you have the room to yourself. I can lay out in my pickup."

"I trust you. I just feel like I've been taking advantage of your hospitality."

"Let's just pretend we're out my way; it's a cold winter night, and you just showed up at my door. I wouldn't turn you away then and I think there's even a better reason not to do it now."

"Do you have a fireplace?" she asked.

"Not at the hotel, but back in Arizona I do."

"Well, never mind then. I'll just stand on this corner and wait until somebody with a fireplace comes by," she said lightly and not even half seriously.

"I have an automatic coffee maker," he announced. "And there's an ice maker down the end of the hall."

"Okay," she smiled and they walked on.

Back at the hotel, after straightening out the sheets and blankets on the bed for Karen, Cody fixed up the faded sofa that he'd sleep on. A cushion here, a couple of rolled up blankets there and it even looked like it wouldn't be too uncomfortable. He let her have one of his King's Ropes tee shirts to sleep in and was surprised how even though it reached down past her thighs, it still revealed the very nice shape she had.

"A finger is a poor excuse for a toothbrush," she said from the bathroom. "I hope you don't mind that I used some of your toothpaste."

"Heck, if I had known two or so weeks ago that I would be (he paused for a split second) sitting with you at the Hotel Earle tonight, I would have packed an extra one," he called back to her.

"Sitting with you?" she said delightedly. "I love the way you choose words. Tell the truth, cowboy, you almost said, 'sleeping' with you,' didn't you?"

"Well, that sort of would be right," he answered. "We are sleeping in the same room, aren't we?"

"That's really cute," she laughed. "If you're talking to my mother you're 'sitting' with me in a hotel room, but when you're back at your Doghouse with your friends in Arizona you were 'sleeping' with me."

After Karen was settled in the bed, Cody stretched himself out on the sofa. He closed his eyes and even though he was very tired he did not fall asleep. There was an uneasiness in his thoughts that kept him awake.

"You know, Karen, I should explain something to you," he said with a little unsteadiness to his voice. "My intentions really were to have you feel safe and protected tonight."

His heartbeat, he thought, grew louder and he was afraid that his heart had become almost visible.

"But also, I realize the wonderful sensuous qualities you have. I'm not sure what you may have thought my intentions were, but I hope you don't think I'm playing games with you."

"You don't have to be anything other than what you are - nice," she said faintly, glancing sideways across her pillow at him.

He searched after words, but what he wanted to say was somehow inexpressible.

They looked at each other and they were pleased with the conversation that was taking place in whispers. They had both forgotten what it was like to actually have the time to talk. There in that night of kindliness they were spellbound.

"My friends used to say I was as wise as a tree full of owls," Cody said barely audible.

"But it seems that that was long ago because I'm having a hard time explaining myself."

"Shhh..." she said. "You don't owe me any explanations."

"I just hate to see someone being nailed into their coffin while their feet are still kicking," Cody said finally. "I think you deserve better than that."

"So do I."

"Believe me," he said with a genuine feeling to the words. "You've made me feel; I don't know if this is going to come out right; you've made me feel that I've sort of known you for a very long time. What I mean, and I say this sincerely, and I know that no woman wants to be compared to another, but you remind me of Sara. And maybe that's one of the real reasons I couldn't let you drive yourself back to your home tonight."

She raised her head off of the pillow and looked across at him sensing his feelings.

"It would be real easy for me to maybe take advantage of what you've been through, but I don't operate that way and I don't want you to make a mistake about me."

"Hey, cowboy," Karen said trying to lighten his awkwardness. "Is this what they call a 'serious conversation'?"

141

"An attempt."

She rose up in the bed and carefully propped the pillows behind her.

"I like you, Cody Stewart; you're refreshing. And if this is a serious conversation then I'm telling you seriously how delighted I am to be here."

Cody looked at her enrapt in her charm.

"When you asked me to stay here tonight I was thrilled. You have no idea how much that invitation meant to me. I would have asked you as a matter of fact if you hadn't asked me. You were absolutely right. The last thing I wanted to do was to go home tonight."

She bit her lip slightly and he could see that she had been trembling.

"I can feel what you've been through, losing someone that you cared so much about. And I certainly don't mind if you think I remind you of Sara. Because from what I can see you were crazy in love with her and you may never get over her. Also, I am not that foolish to think you drove two thousand miles across the country to find a married woman with two children and an extra-marital affair."

"All my life I've kind of lived by some simple rules. One of them was about stealing; I never take another man's property, his saddle, his horse, or his wife. Unfortunately, one of the other rules I live by is that I don't stand by and watch as anyone is abused, especially those that can't defend themselves."

He took a moment to think about the code he had spoken of and then he continued, "There is a big problem, Karen, in that I am wicked attracted to you."

He did not know if she really was asleep or just pretending, but Karen didn't respond to his last remark and he finally closed his eyes not knowing whether she had heard him or not.

Chapter VI

Plans have a way of changing. Af ter breakfast the next morning Cody decided that he would load up his pick up and follow Karen back out to the Long Island to make sure there weren't any problems at home waiting for her.

With the last of his equipment stowed away he suddenly pulled up short.

"I don't believe this," he said. "Of all the cars and trucks and God knows what other kinds of transportation you have in this city, why is it that my tire has to be the one to get baptized?"

Karen saw he was referring to the left front wheel of his Ranger which was now haphazardly spattered and resting comfortably on a yellowish stain beside the curb.

"I swear if I didn't know better I'd think Tom was around. He would do this all the time," Cody reminisced. "Even with all the

Palo Verde trees around the ranch he always found this same tire the best place to leave his mark."

"Maybe he has a relative in the neighborhood," Karen laughed.

"I don't know about that, but I know why Tom loves this tire. It's the word 'Firestone'."

"Oh, Tom can read?"

"That's right. He knows the word 'fire' - really - whether it's written or spoken he knows it. And he knows it's a bad thing and he always lifts his leg whenever he sees it or hears it."

"It must be tough keeping a campfire going at night," she joked.

"You bet. One night I nearly froze to death. And fire flies were even worse. He'd just run around on three legs trying to put them out."

"You are kidding?"

"No, I'm not. Another time he ruined a perfectly good bottle of Jack Daniel's when Poorcrow referred to it as 'firewater'."

"Come on."

"Then there was the time they had one of those 'fire eaters' at one of the rodeos. Well, you can imagine what happened there."

"And just how did you teach him to know

the word 'fire'?"

"Oh, I'm not taking any credit for that. Count me out. It was the firemen," Cody said leaning against the door of the Ford.

"The firemen?"

"Sure, you see when he was a pup he belonged to Billy Brandt's brother, Trey, who was a fireman in Window Rock. Well, anyway, Trey took Tom to the fire station everyday. And around that time there were a lot of suspicious brush fires going on. Well, to make a long story short, because even as a pup he was such a great tracker, he located the 'fire bug'."

"And that's where he developed his technique?"

"Exactly. He mastered the leg lift. But he got carried away. As you can understand there were just too many distractions: the 'fire station', the 'fire engine', the 'fire extinguisher', the 'fire hose', and need I mention all the 'fire hydrants' in Window Rock?"

"Talented puppy! He must have been able to hold a lot of water!"

"'He could. Actually, they say he was able to put out small grass fires by himself, but the havoc he was causing as he grew got to be too much. So, Trey asked around and eventually he became mine," Cody said opening the door and sliding in behind the wheel.

A few minutes later he was following her down F. D. R. Drive out of the city.

The drive along the shore was pleasant. It was another agreeable Indian summer day and the sea was calm with the absence of wind and whitecaps.

The horizon to the east was latticed with fishermen working their nets hoping the good weather would hold. Cody understood the loneliness of their occupation. He could identify with the scarred hands that rope-pulled the catch of the day on to the decks. He also had the clenched wrinkles around the eyes from too much time spent looking into the sun.

Karen's village was a typical Long Island community. The type that each spring would find flowerboxes filled with daffodils and backyards loaded with Dogwood and Lilacs. But now after the leaves had turned and fallen it seemed gray and solemn.

At the mouth of the road leading to her home was a white octagonal house built during the Revolutionary War. After that there were several older homes spread out around a saltmarsh and a few bleached scrub pines.

Approaching her weathered clapboard saltbox he could see a cow lowing in the small pasture behind a barn. As he got closer he could tell that she had not yet been milked that morning.

Karen stopped her car abruptly in the middle of the driveway, flung the door open and began running across the yard towards her house. As she ran she let out a great scream and threw her hands up to her head.

"No! No! Oh God, no!" She cried as she dug her fingers into her scalp and tore at her hair.

In an instant the cowboy was out of his truck chasing after her. He caught up to her as she reached the tree beside the back porch door.

There hanging by her hind legs from one of the tree's limbs was Karen's favorite of her two cows - Isabelle. Her throat had been slashed and the hide removed.

Karen fell to her knees and put her arms around the dead cow's head. She held it to her and ran her fingers along Isabelle's face as if she were a blind woman trying to read it. She felt her ears and mouth and ran her palms over the dead animal's eyes. She was in great pain, sobbing violently, her eyes burning, her mouth disfigured.

"Why? Why? How could he do this? Why?" she cried.

Cody stooped beside her and put his

hands on her shoulders. She turned her head towards him and looked at him with fright. It was like someone had taken her own heart and pushed it straight through her body.

"Oh God! How could he do this to his girls?" she called out in a cry full of fury. "They loved that cow." She was overwhelmed by the sight of Isabelle with her throat cut and her blood spilled upon the soil beneath the tree.

Cody got down slowly on his knees and put his arms around Karen's shoulders. Even though he was aware of the fate of the cattle he had driven across the range, he had never seen anything as monstrous as this. "How could one human being do this to another?" he thought. Isabelle was like a family pet and it hurt him deeply and he had a heartfelt compassion for Karen's grief.

She writhed in pain, seized by the hideous horror before her. Cody took her arms from around the dead animal and lifted her away from it. Partially coagulated blood smeared across her jumper as he slid her away from the carcass which had become heavy and cold.

Her eyes were inflamed and she tried to avoid looking at Cody.

"I don't understand," she said with a shuddering breath.

"I know," Cody said. "I'm sorry."

"Does he hate me that much?"

He turned her face to his. Her face had lost it's fragile prettiness. It had become flooded with grief as she tried to comprehend what had taken place.

"What am I going to do?" she said trying to control herself. "What am I going to tell my children?"

"You'll get through this Karen," he said listening to the anguish in her voice, seeing the sadness in her eyes.

Cody pulled her to him and she surrendered to his arms. Those few minutes, which had seemed like hours of despair, had desperately exhausted her and she became limp as she recognized how merciless her husband, Greg, had been.

"Let me help you inside," Cody said guiding her away from the unbearably frightful scene. He tried the door, but it was locked.

"Above the ledge," Karen whispered hoarsely, letting him know where the key could be found. Cody retrieved it and with one arm around the distraught woman he'd come to care about, he opened the back porch door and they entered the house.

Is it possible to ever reach pain's far bor-

ders? How heavy a penance must a life endure?
Can a heart absorb all the futility that surrounds
it and still beat on with hope?

It had been an awful homecoming, but
now there was more.

Karen's home had been ravaged; every
drawer and closet, every cupboard and bureau,
her cedar chest, her desk and computer, everything that was hers, that she treasured, had been
ransacked. There had been a rampage through
her clothes and possessions. The floors were
littered with blouses and dresses, coats and un-
derwear, socks and shoes, scarves and gloves,
pictures and keepsakes.

Her husband, unable to slake his anger,
had violently devastated her belongings. In the
kitchen pots and pans were strewn along the
floor. Pages were torn from cookbooks. A
drawer full of silverware had been thrown
against a wall. Dishes had been ripped from
an antique hutch that Karen's grandmother had
given her as a wedding present.

In her bedroom her toiletries had been
vindictively dumped out on to her bed. The
comforter had soaked up the fluids and the room
was filled with the sickening combination of
her favorite essences which hung in the gloom.

"He's made it real easy for me," she said
speaking as if she had been waiting for permis-

sion to breathe.

Seeing her home like that was terrifying. Her senses and her mind had been devoured by the frightening sights she'd witnessed. She felt so unprepared, so vulnerable, so confused. Karen tried to control her tears; she was trying to be brave, but it was impossible.

She picked up a toaster from the kitchen floor. One side of it was bent in and an element stuck out. She brought it close to her chest and the tears started to flow.

"How will I make English Muffins in the morning?" she asked Cody sobbing. "My Sarah loves English Muffins and I won't be able to make her any."

"Don't worry about it. Everything is going to be okay," he said trying to comfort her. "We'll get her English Muffins."

"Do you like English Muffins, cowboy?" she asked him.

"Sure," he replied.

"That's good," she said and she walked over and placed the toaster on a kitchen counter. Several times she pulled in her breath, trying to control the sobs, but they broke through anyway.

"I'm usually a better housekeeper than this," she said trying to compose herself.

153

Cody pulled up a stool next to the counter. He removed a pair of flannel pajamas that were draped across the seat. Handing them to her he said, "You know what I think, Karen? I think your clothes had the right idea. Make a break for it! Take that run for freedom. Week after week, month after month held hostage in a closet. I think some of them just wanted to go as far as your clothesline, hang out with their friends, feel the wind down their necks or the sun under a skirt. I don't think Greg did this, I think it was a planned escape."

Karen was smiling through her tears. "What about the silverware and the appliances - the toaster?" she asked slowly, getting tangled up in his clothesline humor.

"They were all turning themselves in as illegal aliens, sneaked over the border one night from Mexico, came in hidden with the Cuban boat people." He paused for a moment and then went on. "I'm sure those knives could tell some stories," he said pointing to a scattered silverware tray against the wall. "Fourteen days at sea in Juan, the sword-swallower's throat. Not a pretty picture."

"And my perfumes?"

"Chemical warfare between France and Belgium that just exploded. No Karen, this disaster was not man made."

"I wish you were right," she sighed uneasily.

"So do I. So do I."

She looked at him and she appreciated how hard he was trying to keep her from going crazy.

"How come you always find the right thing to say?" she asked.

"My explanation is a lot easier to handle than the truth."

"I created a monster," she said with an uncertain laugh. "When Greg realized yesterday, that for the past several months he'd lost control - he lost control. He would have been 'happy' forever if he never found out from the Threadman what kind of woman he had been married to all these years."

"And would you have been 'happy' forever too, Karen?"

"No, but perhaps I'll be 'lonely' forever."

"That's something you'll have a choice in; staying here gives you no choice in the matter at all."

Slowly and deliberately, Karen picked up a couple of overturned chairs and some of the silverware.

"I really appreciate your being so straight-forward-honest with me, Cody."

155

"Listen, Karen, all I know is that what I've seen here in your home and outside today is, to my way of thinking, about as cruel as it gets. And I know that if life doesn't teach us to be fair, then it teaches us nothing. If anything, I've learned something immeasurably more valuable, and far more full of meaning these past few days than I realized." His voice became direct and serious. "I've discovered that 'used' is the only four letter word that becomes worse when you put 'AB' before it."

"Believe me, it's a long painful process," she replied, stealing a nervous glance at him.

"Well, I do have one question for you," he said taking her glance and holding it.

She looked at him with the slightest apprehension.

"What can I do to help you with all this?" he asked her, his voice soft with reflective warmth.

There was a moment of silence, then almost childlike, she said hesitantly, "Would I be asking too much to have you bury Isabelle out back in the pasture? I don't think I can go back out that way with her still hanging there."

She was on the verge of tears again.

"Sure," he said. "I'll back up the truck and cut her down into it. Don't worry; everything is going to be all right."

"Thank you," she said as her lips quivered a little and moisture welled up in her eyes.

Jim McBride

Chapter VII

Karen's land was divided into two small meadows separated by cedar post fencing that extended along the far side of her barn out towards a sleeve of scrub pines.

The limpid light of the morning was occasionally broken by gulls scavenging away from the shore. Every now and again one would call out as it glided by before hooking into a curve and disappearing into the distance.

There next to the grove, below the unharnessed gulls of the sky, Cody buried the cow.

A short while after he had finished and was returning her tools to the barn, Karen came down off of the porch steps from where she had been watching. She had changed her clothes and was wearing a pair of stained trousers and her hair was tucked up under a woolen baseball cap.

She met him near the milking parlor where her daughters' bicycles rested, their tires mud-splattered from recent rides into the village.

"Hi," she said. Then, "Thanks again."

"How are you doing?" he asked her.

"I straightened up inside as much as I could, but I've really got to get Irene milked."

"I'll go get her for you if you like," he said pleasantly.

"It's not necessary." She opened the door to the outside where the cow was browsing in the pasture and called, "Reenie, Reenie! Come on girl. Come on!" She picked up a bucket and banged her open palm against it. "Come on Reenie!"

Irene made her way across the field and clumped into the milking parlor. Karen placed her into the milking stand and filled the bucket beneath it with some of Irene's favorite treats so that while she was emptying down at her udder, she was also filling up her rumen.

Karen worked her fingers against the teats and as each squirt hit the stainless steel bucket it echoed through the small room until it was filled with warm fresh milk.

Cody stood there watching her, the light filtering into the room behind him came in

shafts as it passed through the dust from the
hay loft.

As Karen milked he became enchanted
with the way she cared for the animal. She
talked softly to Irene, encouraging her, tenderly
telling her not to be sad, recalling recollections
and old impressions of her days with Isabelle.
Cody's feeling was that she was also comforting herself. He could see she was unaccustomed
to carrying around a swollen heart and during
those moments she struggled to smile weakly
back at him, but he could tell she was suffocat-
ing.

"There was a time, a million years ago,
that I really was involved in the way the world
was going," she said as she strained the fresh
milk into another container. "I did the whole
thing: marches on Washington, letters to anyone who mattered, even organic foods. But then
as time wore on I realized I couldn't save the
whole wide world, so I thought maybe if I could
just save my few acres of land that would be a
start." She climbed a couple of rungs up the
ladder to the hayloft. "I hoped that people all
over would do the same thing and eventually
we could get it all taken care of," she said looking down at Cody.

"There's nothing wrong with that."

"I wanted to help, one human being to

161

another." She grabbed a bale of hay, handed it to him and made her way back down.

"Let me get that door, cowboy."

She opened the door and he took the bale and brought it out to the hay crib.

"So much for idealism. I couldn't even help myself," she said walking beside him.

They went back in and Cody climbed up, grabbed another bale and brought it out.

"The way I see it, Karen, you can carry this hay out one bale or one straw at a time. And I think the same thing applies to a person's life. It depends upon how much you can take, how much you want to carry and for how long."

"Put me down for one straw, magnified a few thousand times," she said. And then she added, "And one trip too many."

The barn was quiet except for a few late season flies still buzzing freely in the dust that had been raised by the pulled bale.

"Only one thing worries me," Karen said regretfully.

Cody looked at her as her face flushed.

"Everything," she said almost inaudibly as a tear untangled itself from her lashes. "Maybe I'm just one of those people bound to lose no matter how hard I try."

"You're no loser, Karen; don't even think

like that."

"I can't help it. What have I done?"

"You've done nothing."

"Nice try, cowboy, but we both know that's not true," she said evenly. "I was carrying on with the Threadman, a guy I really couldn't even stand. What does that make me?"

"It doesn't make you anything," he replied. "You know what I think, Karen? I think that was your first step out of your marriage, a step you knew you had to take."

"Then why do I feel so humiliated?" she asked.

"Because that's what Greg wants you to feel. If he drinks it's because you've driven him to it. If he hits you it's because you've made him so angry he doesn't know what else to do. He wants you to feel you've caused everything, that you're the one responsible."

Cody looked at her with the unmistakable feeling that there was a real affection growing between them.

"How come you're so nice to me?" she asked. "Are you an angel?" she said smiling through damp eyes.

"No, I'm just normal. I hope that's not too big a disappointment."

They were both silent.

163

She had a very beautiful face, even in her sadness and for a long time he looked into her eyes without saying a word."

"Disappointment?" she said finally in a faltering voice.

Cody saw she was close to weeping.

"You ride in from the west, your shining armor as bright as the sun and you think I'm disappointed? No, cowboy, I'm not disappointed if you're not really an angel, or Sir Lancelot from the Round Table. If I'm disappointed in anything it's that last night when you said you were 'attracted' to me, I pretended to be asleep."

She rose up on tiptoes and took his face in her hands and kissed him. Then she whispered into his ear, "Thank you for your kindness."

As the word "kindness" came forth so did her tears. It was a word that touched the secret in her heart. It was the relief of having been able to say the word that brought on the tears. That word had been missing for so long from her life and now here was this man from out west bringing it to her, with no attachments.
"Hey, it's all right," Cody said putting his arms around her, feeling the slight tremble that ran through her.

"I work in a city of millions and still I've

been lonely," she said. "I've been without tenderness, gentleness, and kindness for so long I've forgotten how comforting they could be."

Karen hesitated for a moment and then between sobs she said, "When you go, cowboy, would you be so good as to leave a little piece of you behind? I need the memory."

She started crying uncontrollably now.

"I don't know," she said trying to compose herself. "Sometimes I'm thinking about other things, then I'm not. I bring up a lot of stuff. My God, how'd I get into all of this?"

Her voice was quivering. She made an attempt to stop weeping, but couldn't.

"I'm sorry. You have no obligation to me."

"It's okay. It's okay," he said gently.

"That's what friends are for."

"Am I really your friend?"

"Of course."

"I'm sorry. I don't want you to see me like this. I don't want you not to like me."

"Hey, let's back up a minute. You don't have to worry about your making me like or not like you. Underneath this Resistol is my own head and I make my own decisions. Believe it or not between these two ears, that hold up this hat, there's still a little gray matter left."

"Resist all?" she said as a slight grin tried to break out across her face. "Is that what this does?" Karen removed the hat from his head and hung it over a halter on one of the wall pegs. "It helps you resist anyone that might be hoping to get close to you?"

"Actually, it's just supposed to cover up 'hat hair'," he replied, glad that he saw a smile breaking through. "In either case it's not working very well anymore."

Karen's eyes shone. There was a blossoming within her. She felt herself grow warm as she looked into the eyes of the man who had befriended her.

Cody felt the same excitement taking hold and forcefully opening his heart. There, deep in that fissure within his heart, came a new light driving away the ache that once was as black as midnight. Emerging slowly and noiselessly the light splintered and scattered all the humdrum bits of routine he had mastered over the years to protect himself.

And then it happened.

Along with the light came a voice barely above a whisper, but at once remembered. A resurrection. Sara spoke to him again.

"Stop beating yourself up, Cody," she told him gently. "We are here only for a wink. Learn to love again." And then her voice slipped away into silence.

A distant belfry chimed twelve.

This time it was Cody who carefully reached forward and took Karen's face in his hands. She stood motionless. The contact with his hands made her feel even warmer. He examined her face closely, in great detail. He saw how her lashes hung down over her eyes, long and beautifully dark. He took his left hand away and brought the pointing finger back to his own lips almost as if telling her not to speak. Simultaneously, she tilted her head slightly to the right, cradling her cheek in his other palm.

Slowly, with a pleasant joy, she kissed the finger which rested perpendicularly across her lips. She was surprised at how delicate it was, but also she felt its strength and masculinity. She brought her hands up to his and took hold of them, all the while looking into the cowboy's eyes.

Karen began to feel happy. She realized that this man had reawakened understanding and friendship within her.

He had listened to her patiently without embarrassing her or making her feel foolish.

As Cody looked into her eyes he wondered how a man like her husband could have become so evil. What must have been taking place in Greg over the years to bring about such hateful antagonism towards so beautiful and healthy a woman like Karen? Neglectfulness, jealousy, suspicions? What fueled and inflamed his bitterness and brought about the estrangement? It had been a long siege for Karen and the final battle had been waged today.

Cody returned from the shadowed portal of his thoughts. As though under a spell he brought his mouth closer to hers until he could smell and feel her warmth and scent like something so familiar. Then with grateful fingers he brought her face to his and drawing her to him he gently kissed her.

For Karen it was like Christmas at Rockefeller Center when the lights on the tree had just been lit and the air was crisp with its brilliance. It was the scream of a hook and ladder through the streets of Manhattan. It was the steam up from a manhole cover in front of Grand Central Station.

For Cody it was like the smell of mesquite and the glow of the slow burning fire. It was the howl of the wind through the cottonwood trees. It was the spray from a fast moving stream.

She was Cinderella a minute before midnight.

He was the Prince of Broken Hearts on the mend.

She was the passenger in the runaway stagecoach and he was the hero in the white hat racing along side.

Karen's eyes were curious and trusting. Her mouth was soft and moist and greeted his again, returning the same friendliness as his first kiss. She looked at him and he saw how beautiful she was and he was absorbed in her joy.

Cody loved the scent that emanated from her skin. It mingled with the smell of the sweet hay from the loft.

Karen held on to his hand and at the same time he could feel her heart pulling him to her. He was surprised how easily she was able to perform this magic. It was incomprehensible how he was being devoured by the jaws of passion that had opened before him. He was delighted with the delicious taste of her smiling lips - so welcoming, so hospitable.

She was comforted by his voice which was soft and sensual like a lullaby. She stroked his hand lightly and happily and let her fingers play among his.

Outside they could here Irene rummage and low as she munched the feed that had been placed before her.

Karen's face shone brightly in the filtered

169

sunlight, content to be kissed and touched sub-
tly and lovingly. There in that moment it came
upon him, an avalanche that silenced any
thoughts or questions he could have ever had.
Words flew from his heart that no longer needed
or deserved definition - Integrity, Intention, Re-
jection, Possession, Surrender, Temptation.
The evidence was revealed in Karen's eyes, in-
timate and accepting. The desire was revealed
in the one word she spoke, "Please."

Somewhere in the back of his heart one
door slammed closed as another opened softly.

"Don't be sorry, Karen," he said quietly,
almost as if giving her the opportunity to re-
tract the word.

When Cody spoke Karen stared into his
light blue eyes, her fingers still laced between
his. She dug with earnestness into her soul for
half a moment and said nothing more, for nothing at all had to be said. She untangled her
fingers, placed her hands behind his neck and
with simple childlike strength drew his mouth
back to hers.

This time her lips seemed to shiver open
and as she squeezed his neck she made an en-
chanting, luring sound in her throat which
unknotted him from his memories.

Cody's heart was like tinder and the fire
in his blood pulsed feverishly through his veins

towards conflagration.

Karen's senses were excited. Her mouth surrendered to his tongue with unbearable delight. She held it and she offered no resistance to Cody's exploration.

She was strangely transformed, rejuvenated with a touching sensuality into a beautiful sexual being who for so long had been enmeshed in passion's abstinence.

He kissed her eyes and mouth and cheeks. He looked at her and memorized her features in detail.

He loved the hollows of her cheeks and saw how they sort of created a corridor up to her high cheek bones. Her skin was light, especially around her eyes except where it became darker in the pocket-corners at the bridge of her nose.

In the shadowy filtered corner of the barn, Karen's eyes looked softly beautiful and shining like the picture of an Egyptian Pharaoh he'd seen in a museum a long time ago. He could see in them the quietness of the mountains around Window Rock and the calmness of a shallow cove where the mustangs watered in summer.

The slow lingering of each pleasant kiss, the possession and absorption brought a great warmth to Karen. She knew she could never grow cold again. His kisses were like little slivers of crusts being offered to a shivering, starving beggar. At first she took them one by one, but even then she had been cold and desperately hungry. Her greediness grew until taking all he could offer her made her unbearably happy.

For many years Cody had thought that trying to have a moment like this again in his life would be like trying to prevent himself from having the same dream he had night after night.

For Karen each of Cody's kisses replaced the birthday or anniversary cards that Greg had always forgotten to buy. Each caress replaced the evenings out to dinner that she hadn't known for years.

Cody unbuttoned each button on her shirt and slid his hands inside, up along the walls of her rib cage. He let his palms rest there at the sides of her breasts feeling every exhalation from deep within her. With each breath her passion rose as Cody began slow fingertip explorations across her breasts.

Gently he let the pads of his fingers skim over her nipples until the slight pressure caused them to become erect. Then pushing the sides of the front of her shirt open he brought his lips to the same area his fingers had explored.

His touch elicited from her a brief quiver of delight. From deep in her throat came a barely perceptible joyful murmur. There was a shimmering kind of glow to her widening eyes as Cody softly let his tongue run over her breasts.

Tenderly and delicately, silently and gratefully Karen received his caresses and kisses. She put her hands around his neck and clung to him delighted by his confidence and care and her awakening sensuality.

As Cody lay her down on to the hay a slight breeze moved through Karen's hair and it reminded him of the wind moving and rippling through fields of wheat on the prairie.

There in the tousled bedding he wrapped himself in the arms of the straw-blond young woman, entangled and absorbed in sheets and blankets of hay. Two sprawled out figures, like laughing children, spellbound and uncompromising, played in the coarse timothy

Beneath it all Karen felt like melting ice, a liquid fugitive running away from solitary confinement. She felt wonderful.

Cody slid his hands down to her work boots, untied the laces and removed them. He rubbed his hands over the blue and white snowflaked socks she was wearing.

173

"Going skiing?" he asked her taking them off. Her feet were warm and they felt familiar and comfortable as he caressed her arches to the backs of the heels.

"I hope it's not all 'down hill' from here," Karen retorted.

"I don't know whether I'm working my way down from the top of the mountain to the lodge base in the valley or taking the chair lift up to Paradise," Cody cajoled.

"I'm not sure either," Karen said looking at Cody who seemed at that moment to be Robert Redford caught between *Jeremiah Johnson* and *The Downhill Racer,* "but don't stop now!"

"You are a very beautiful woman, Karen," he whispered lifting his eyes to hers.

Soundlessly Karen removed his shirt and then unloosened the gold and silver buckle with the saddle bronc rider, from his Wranglers. Cody quickly pulled off his boots, socks, and pants in record time.

"4.2 seconds," he said throwing up his hands as if in mock calf roping competition.

Before she could finish laughing he was once again entangled with her, pulling her hips to him, kissing her and lovingly caressing her secret delight with soft and delicate strokes.

"That's very nice," she murmured between kisses, catching her breath.

"I'm not hurting you, am I?" he asked.

"You are very rare. How is it that you seem to know what I need? Especially when it's something I thought I'd always want but would never be able have?"

Karen loved the way he was touching her with his fingers, cautiously penetrating the hidden alcoves of her nature. She was mesmerized by the cowboy's curiosity and the discoveries he was making. He loved the way her body responded to his touch and the delightful moisture that magically coated his fingers and hand.

Like two dancers shawled in the gauzy stable light, they gathered and clung and felt the growing warmth. Slowly and sensually they rediscovered that tattered lost realm of innocence. Together with each kiss and caress they retreated into the iridescent glow, the promising paradise that surrounded them. There lost in the strewn about patches of hay, Cody carefully and lovingly threaded the eye of the needle he had found and repaired the fabric of their souls.

"Thank you," she said opening her eyes and seeing that it had all been real.

"For what? Being in love with you?" he replied kindly.

He had said it. It was a word she had not heard in a long while, a word he had truthfully only spoken to one other person in his life.

For an instant Cody recalled how two summers ago he had roped a chestnut stallion down near the riverside. He remembered how the mustang circled him, eyeing him as he kept shortening the circle, keeping the slant of the rope taut. Cody knew then, by the look in the horse's eyes, that the animal would rather it's heart burst than be taken in. The cowboy remembered how he braced his boots in the stirrups and hung back against the cantle when the stallion charged. He saw the desperation in his eyes, the strength in his shoulders and back, and he could still feel the impact of when the mustang closed on him with the true truth.

Karen had propped herself up docilely on an elbow and was looking at the man from out west. A little smile remained loyal to her face and her eyes were laced with wonder. She had a newfound ecstasy within her and a strong sense of having become intensely feminine.

"I will always remember October 12th," she said almost as if she would be helpless to do otherwise.

Cody smiled at her as she continued. "Because for a short hour around noon I threw off the claustrophobic blanket that I'd been wearing for so long."

There had been a great, almost chemical, reaction between them. Like two dull precious coins that had been allowed to tarnish over time, they now both gleamed and flashed. And each of them held the other close like their own last valuable possession. A silver-tinted aura surrounded them, brighter than a hundred moonlights spangling across their naked bodies. It seeped down into their souls and flowed medicinally to the cornerstones of their hearts.

Chapter VIII

The seabirds circled overhead like their distant cousins in the west and Cody Stewart made his way through the gate of the chain-linked fence on to the tennis courts. His hat was pulled down hard and he looked out from beneath the dark brim that shaded his eyes towards the man at the other end.

Standing at the far baseline was the man he'd seen at Morgan's a few days earlier, Larry the Threadman, the man who had made Karen's life so miserable. He was hitting backhand and forehand topspin returns back at the serving machine Cody was walking behind.

Cody stopped and stood there watching the Threadman's strokes, each ball coming back deep into the service court. Cody waited there, his eyes narrowed like a gunfighter's, watching the tennis player swing hard through the balls, and deliver them within feet of where the

179

cowboy waited.

Every ten seconds or so the machine shot a ball out at the Threadman and every ten second or so a ball rocketed back closer and closer to the cowboy.

"May I be of help to you?" Larry said facetiously calling out to Cody between strokes.

"From what I understand that would be a first for you, Larry. It's my understanding that you're only interested in helping yourself."

"Is that what Greg's wife told you?" he said emphasizing "Greg's wife" and pulling his racket up and over a ball and driving it hard near Cody's boot.

"Karen didn't have to tell me anything, Larry. I've never had any problems recognizing a snake."

Cody had moved a yard inside the baseline and the next ball off of the Threadman's racket took a quick hop to his left. The cowboy, with a deft reflex, caught the yellow orb, examined the "Penn 4" on it and rolled it forward into the net.

"You'll have to do better than that, Threadman." Cody smiled back at him and took a couple of steps forward into the playing area.

The next return skidded when it hit and angled into Cody's body. Again he deftly

stepped to the side and backhanded it much the
same way he did when fielding ground balls for
Coach Schiffner at Window Rock High years
ago.

Once more he rolled the ball in his left
hand into the net and stepped a yard closer

At the mention of the name "Threadman",
Larry started to slowly turn pale, the blood
draining from his face as he bit down hard on
his tongue. He tried to drive the next ball right
at Cody, but this time the man from Arizona
squared to the ball and caught the line drive
right above the gold buckle he'd won in Kansas. Again he looked the ball over and then
mechanically rolled it slowly into the net.

"Where's Karen's husband?" Cody asked
from the service line, halfway to the net.

The next ball was miss hit by the
Threadman and sailed well over Cody's head
and clanged against the fence.

"You seem to play tennis about as well
as you sing," Cody said smiling.

Those words came to the Threadman as
hard as the balls he'd been hitting at Cody. He
knew then that Karen had told the cowboy everything, and he continued to blanch.

"You seem a bit nervous, Larry, something I said?"

"You don't scare me, cowboy."

"I'm not here to scare you, Larry. If I were here to do that I would have been over the net already unraveling your twine."

The Threadman smashed another ground stroke back at the cowboy who quickly snatched it out of the air and nonchalantly flipped it behind his back into the net and stepped up to within two yards of the net.

"Let me ask you," Larry said with false bravado, "Did she tell you how she was planning to leave Greg and marry me before you came along?" He hit another shot towards Cody's left ear and once again Cody's hand shot up and seized the missile and dropped it softly on to the court.

Cody knew that what the Threadman was saying was a lie because Karen had told him about the situation earlier in the week.

"A word of advice, Larry. If you don't have the fangs, don't shake your rattle."

Because Cody had left the gate open it was easy for Greg, who had just arrived, to enter the court without being seen by the cowboy. The hum of the Ace Master machine, plus the continual contact of the balls with the racket covered up any sound he might have made coming across the court.

182

Knowing now that he was no longer alone, and that the odds had gotten more to his liking, Larry got braver.

"So, have you been screwing her long, cowboy?" he said cockily, more for Greg's benefit than his own.

"You know, Larry, if I were you I'd find a hole or a rock and start slithering towards it."

"That won't be necessary," he said slamming another forehand volley at Cody who stabbed it as it whizzed by his shoulder.

By this time Greg had moved up to about five or six yards behind the cowboy. He put his bag down and quietly took out the composite racket he used. It was one of those models with the oversized head put out by Donnay, and he knew he'd probably be able to get in a couple of good whacks at Cody's head with it.

The former Window Rock High baseball pitcher still held the last ball that the Threadman had hit at him in his hand. He flipped it into his right hand. He fingered it the way he had been taught: thumb directly under, fingers across the seams. It actually felt good to hold a ball in his throwing hand again. For a second he remembered how he used to throw stones at the trees at Bailey's Pond with Sara, after he had given up the idea of going to

A. S. U. She would pick out a spot he'd let fly, and the stone would land usually right on the money.

The Threadman was trying to be loose. He held his racket before him, cutting the air out in front of his chest with a slicing motion, while he waited for the next ball from the machine. Seeing Greg silently coming up behind the cowboy made Larry's mouth slide comfortably into a turned-up grin.

"Something funny, Larry?" the cowboy asked.

"Just you, Tex," he retorted, his smile widening.

"Bet it's not as funny as it's going to be when you step on that loose shoelace," Cody replied, pointing down at the Threadman's feet.

It was at the quick of that moment that the Threadman lowered his racket to look at his feet, when Cody reached back and cocked his arm behind him. Years of practice through Little League and Senior League, High School and American Legion baseball were combined in that throw. It all came back to him in that instant: plant the landing foot, pull the back leg through, turn the torso, get the head out over the front knee, let the rocket go.

"Made you look," Cody chuckled as the ball reached its target and went into the

Threadman's groin like a sword.

Involuntarily, Larry doubled over, his feet stumbled looking for anchorage; he tumbled on to the court blinded by the pain.

Cody Stewart, high school pitching phenom, had always had the confidence to spot his fastball wherever he wanted.

"Didn't anyone ever tell you to wear a cup no matter what sport you played?" he asked stolidly.

The Threadman was gasping for air, bewildered, trying to hold the family jewels together with both hands. He writhed in agony, his eyes rolling as his head wobbled and he turned on to his back.

As the ball exploded into the Threadman Greg stepped up behind Cody and started what he thought would be a well placed crack to the back of the cowboy's head. But then, right as his racket was starting its descent, from out of nowhere came a low guttural growl followed by a black and white blur which flew through the air.

Cody turned and watched as in a kind of slow-motion, from God only knows where, came a deep snarl and his long-time companion and cowdog, Tom. He sounded mean; he looked mean; and he bit mean. In that thou-

sandth of a second Tom's jaws snapped on
Karen's husband's forearm and the momentum
of the leap drove both man and dog off at an
angle, causing the intended blow to fall wide
of Cody.

Meanwhile, on the other side of the net
the Threadman was lying flat on his back, still
in excruciating pain, as every ten seconds the
practice machine shot balls into him.

Having knocked him away from his master, Tom stood looking at Greg in a menacing
way. He remained alert, his ears laid back and
his tail held high. But it was Cody, far more
quickly then Greg had expected, who was over
him grabbing him by the collar of his Fila shirt
and lifting him up on to his feet.

"Is that how you did it to Isabelle, Greg?
Snuck up behind her?" Cody said, the words
burning in his throat.

"Take your hands off of me!" he yelled
grimacing.

"I thought I had seen the worst," Cody
said, twisting the shirt collar tighter around
Greg's throat. A spasm of fear went through
Karen's husband.

"You had your chance and you blew it,
Greg. You'll never hurt her again," Cody said
to him in a sheet of anger.

"Who the hell are you? What do you think you're doing?" Greg choked out.

"I'm the guy who's going to let you feel what it's like to be abused." And with that he took his free hand and slapped Karen's husband open handed along the side of his head. "That was for the time at the beach. Remember, The time you held her head under because she couldn't run anymore?"

The right side of Greg's face turned cranberry where the slap had landed.

Greg tried to throw a feeble hook at the cowboy who blocked it and slapped him hard again, causing some blood to trickle from Greg's nose.

"I thought you were a tough guy, Greg. Is that the best you can do? I thought you city guys were supposed to be mean?"

Greg looked at Cody meekly, the cowboy's left hand still pressing hard against his throat.

"This is for the burnt hand." And again Cody slapped him. This time it was a backhand to the other side of Greg's face.

Karen's husband was completely frightened now and his fear made him absolutely helpless.

"You know what's sad, Greg?" Cody said

almost under his breath. "What's sad is that I don't have as much time to do to you what you've done to Karen."

Tears welled up in Greg's eyes.

"Oh, I know all about your past. I know all about Karen's hurts and scars."

The area around Greg's left eye was skinned and swollen.

"You're a very stupid man, Greg, stupid and evil. You drove a perfectly beautiful and caring woman away, a woman who would have been faithful to you to the end if you could have shown her the least bit of kindness."

Cody grabbed him by the hair and turned his head towards the far court where Larry was still laid out on his back.

"You let a fine woman get involved with that," Cody said gesturing with his head towards the Threadman. And then you let that garbage bring disgrace upon her in front of your pastor," Cody said between clenched teeth, his hand trembling as he held on to Greg.

Cody was having a great amount of difficulty with his restraint. His control was ebbing within him as he thought of what Greg and the Threadman had put Karen through. If there was one thing in life that the cowboy hated more than any thing it was inequity. He resented unfairness especially when those being treated unjustly had no defense against it.

"You know, Greg, it's been said that a man who abuses his wife is like the coyote in the chicken coop: once he's gotten the taste for it he can't be cured. But be assured. I'm going to try my darndest to prove that untrue."

And with that Cody released his hands from Greg's throat and hair and then lightening-like clapped them together on either side of Greg's head.

Greg's head reeled from the savageness of the blows. His already damp eyes burned and his ears rang as if the lightening strike had started a fire which was now roaring wildly. through his head. Stunned, he fell backward. Terrified, he knew there was no hope for him. He was at the complete mercy of the man from Arizona.

A true friendship existed between the cowdog and his master, so until Tom felt there was no longer any threat or danger to Cody he did not let himself become enraptured with the machine that spit balls out like gunfire. For the past several minutes he had ignored and totally disregarded those yellow objects that flew across the court at the Threadman. But now the urge to investigate became too great.

Joyously he bounded towards the marvel-

ous device which seemed to be set upon a min-
iature windmill. Besides being the excellent
tracker he had proven himself to be, he was also
a smart dog. It did not take more than an couple
of minutes for Tom to figure out that as long
as he retrieved the balls and replaced them into
the hopper of the automatic feeder, they would
continue to shoot across the net and hit the
Threadman.

For Tom this was great fun, almost as
much fun as fetching a stick that had been
thrown into Bailey's Pond on Summer's hot-
test day.

Gregory Woodward cast an anxious look
at the cowboy. It was the first time in his life
that anything like this had ever happened to
him. He got himself maneuvered around into a
kind of sitting position as he tried to blend into
his shadow which rolled out behind him.

Everything had happened at once - the
pain, the astonishment - all from the lightening snaps of punishment that his head had
yielded to. Spark-like implosions still flashed
behind his eyes. He tried to somehow bring
sense to the unstable equilibrium he was experiencing. Greg Woodward had forfeited bravado; he knew fear and Cody Stewart saw it in
his face.

The cowboy remembered how Billy

Brandt had taught him how to forefoot and throw a mustang in order to break him. He recalled the look in the animal's eyes and now he saw it again in the face of Karen's husband.

Looking down into Greg's face the cowboy felt the danger within himself of letting another surge of rage overcome him. He knew anger was quick to feed upon itself and if he did not curb that fierceness, right then, he could become just like the man cowering before him.

The enmity within Cody Stewart was like a skittish animal he was trying to get under control. It was deeply embedded and persisted in dragging up all the reasons why he should give the man, with the fear in his eyes, an even greater convincing. Thankfully, from somewhere far off, sameness came and weeded the growing garden of contempt.

Cody drew a breath. He had come, he knew, pretty close to letting Greg win, but regardless of all that the man evoked within him, Cody had been able to stop. And that is what he did. He whistled once for his cowdog on the other side of the court and together they walked towards the chainlink gate, never once looking back.

Epilogue

And so Cody Stewart headed back to Window Rock. He did not fall over the flat edge of the Earth, even though he had come close.

"Was getting across the George Washington Bridge going to be the hardest part of my trip home?" Cody thought to himself as the miles of traffic inched its way over the Hudson River. It seemed that every twenty feet or so the pickup paused as vehicles funneled into a single line around the road repairs going on. No vehicle was exempt; none could disentangle itself from the long beaded chain.

Before him a horsethief moon started its assent over the New Jersey Palisades and the bright halogen lights of the night crew came on. In the back of the pickup Tom lay alongside Cody's saddle and equipment bag with his chin resting sleepily across his paw. This trip was certainly going to be more pleasant and comfortable than the one he'd taken earlier to find his master.

In the few short miles since they had left Long Island, Tom had even been able to come to terms with Irene, Karen's cow, who looked over the side of the pickup at the hard-hatted construction workers with wonder

It had been a simple decision. He had said many times since Sara's death that he could "endure pain, but not loss." But now he had come to realize something else about himself during his stay in the east - nothing could be more painful than regret.

Inside the cab Karen held on to Cody's hand as tightly as she did when they drove out of her driveway for the last time. Her two girls, Sarah and Teresa, slept peacefully, leaning their heads against their mother's shoulders.

At the bridge's border sign that separates New York from New Jersey an iron worker directing traffic around the repair area peered into the truck at its occupants.

"Nice family you've got there, cowboy," he said smiling at the girls and the animals on board.

"Thank you, thank you very much," Cody replied grinning back at him knowing that what he'd said was absolutely true.

-The End-

Be sure to read Jim McBride's first book,
THE CLEARING

Here is what critics have to say . . .

Boston Sunday Herald, "Much like the sentimental 'Bridges of Madison County,' this melodramatic, though sweet-natured love story brings two romantic souls together for a short, but magical time amid the pressure of outside obligations."

Cape Cod Times, "A tender taut tale of love and mystery spanning the centuries between the pilgrim era and our own."

Romantic Times, "McBride is a poetic, sensuous writer. More literary than mainstream, THE CLEARING is for those who want a different paranormal read . . ."

Chuck Potter, WSUB radio, "McBride uses the language like a concert violinist to wend through time and emotion, delivering you to, as the title says, a romantic clearing in your heart and mind. THE CLEARING is an artful romance novel that you will probably finish too quickly."

William Gibson, author of THE MIRACLE WORKER, "McBride's tongue is gifted with a kind of Irish gaeity, witty and charming."

Diana N. Fabbri, WOMR, "Jim McBride opens the window that looks out upon the clearing and brings us hope and a love that lasts forever."